あまつかぜ

Heaven's Wind

A dual language anthology of contemporary Japanese writing

Kuniko Mukoda
Natsuko Kuroda
Kaori Ekuni
Mitsuyo Kakuta
Aoko Matsuda

Edited and translated by **Angus Turvill**

The Japan Society

First published 2018 by
The Japan Society
13/14 Cornwall Terrace
London NW1 4QP
www.japansociety.org.uk

ISBN: 978-0-9559977-2-3

Designed and set by Atsushi Takamura

Printed in the UK by Henry Ling Limited

Contents

Introduction

This anthology brings together the work of five remarkable Japanese authors. Three are winners of the Naoki Prize and one a winner of the Akutagawa Prize. They were born over five decades, from 1929 to 1979. All of them happen to be women.

The pieces themselves were written between 1963 and 2012. The fictional worlds they portray are set against pre-war to present-day backdrops, taking in town, countryside, suburb and coast. They engage with themes of childhood and child loss, work and society, marriage and isolation, deceit, illness and disaster.

The stories are presented in Japanese and English translation, in a parallel-text format. It is hoped that they will be enjoyed by readers of either language. The translations are designed to be read as independent texts, and are not word-by-word guides to the Japanese originals. It is, nevertheless, hoped that anybody reading in the language in which they are less proficient will be able to get some useful prompts by glancing at the facing page. To help learners of Japanese, phonetic guides for all kanji characters are given in the Japanese texts. Readings of some Japanese words can vary according to time and place. Where possible the readings specified in this book are based on the authors' own preferences or suggestions.

A commentary by the translator at the end of the book summarises some of the ways in which the Japanese texts are affected by the translation process. Several of the translations have won prizes or commendations in major translation competitions, so it is hoped that the analysis may be of interest to those involved in the practice of Japanese translation.. It is also hoped that general readers will be interested in how and why the original texts and translations differ.

The anthology's title, *Heaven's Wind,* is a reference to a poem by Sojo Henjo (僧正遍昭) (816-890), one of the six great poets of the early Heian period.

あまつかぜ	amatsukaze
くものかよひぢ	kumo no kayoiji
ふきとぢよ	fukitojiyo
をとめのすがた	otome no sugata
しばしとどめむ	shibashi todomen

This might tentatively be translated as follows:

Blow, heaven's wind
Close up
The pathway through the clouds
And keep the maidens
Here a while

We hope that this anthology will help to keep these wonderful Japanese authors in readers' minds for many years to come.

向田邦子　Kuniko Mukoda

1929年東京生まれ。作家としての活動とともに、人気テレビ、ラジオドラマの脚本家として活躍。英語で読むことのできる作品に短編集『The Name of the Flower（花の名前）』がある。「かわうそ」は1980年に他の二作品とともに直木賞を受賞している。1981年、台湾旅行中に飛行機事故のため逝去。「かわうそ」の英訳は、2006年ジョン・ドライデン翻訳コンクールの準優賞受賞作に基づく。

Kuniko Mukoda was born in Tokyo in 1929. Besides her literary output, she was a leading scriptwriter of television and radio dramas. She has one collection of stories available in English: *The Name of the Flower*. 'Kawauso' ('The Otter') is one of three stories for which she was awarded the Naoki Prize in 1980. She was killed in an air crash in Taiwan in 1981. This English version of 'The Otter' is based on a prize-winning entry to the 2006 John Dryden Translation Competition.

かわうそ

The Otter

向田邦子

Kuniko Mukoda

指先から煙草が落ちたのは、月曜の夕方だった。

宅次は縁側に腰かけて庭を眺めながら煙草を喫い、妻の厚子は座敷で洗濯物をたたみながら、いつものはなしを蒸し返していたときである。

二百坪ばかりの庭にマンションを建てる建てないで、夫婦は意見がわかれていた。厚子は不動産屋のすすめに乗って建てるほうにまわり、宅次は停年になってからでいいじゃないかと言っていた。停年にはまだ三年あった。

植木道楽だった父親の遺したものだけに、うちは大したことないが、庭だけはちょっとしたものである。宅次は勤めが終わると真直ぐうちへ帰り、縁側に坐って一服やりながら庭を眺めるのが毎日のきまりになっていた。

暦をめくるように、季節で貌を変える庭木や下草、ひっそりと立つ小さな五輪の石塔が、薄墨に溶け夜の闇に消えてゆくのを見ていると、一時間半の通勤も苦に思えなかった。文書課長という、出世コースからはずれた椅子も腹が立たなかった。おれの本当の椅子は、この縁側だという気がしていた。

The cigarette fell from his fingertips one Monday evening.

He was sitting on the veranda, looking at the garden. The sliding screen that separated the house and veranda was open, and Atsuko, his wife, was kneeling in the tatami-matted room inside, folding the washing. She had yet again raised the contentious issue of whether to build on the garden.

Atsuko had been convinced it was a good idea by the estate agent. It was a decent-sized plot and big enough for an apartment block. Takuji resisted, saying they might as well wait until he retired. That was three years away.

The house was nothing to speak of, but the garden was rather fine. Takuji had inherited the place from his father, a man whose indulgence was trees and plants. Each day after work, Takuji would come straight home and sit on the veranda with his cigarette, looking at the garden. He enjoyed observing how the vegetation changed with the seasons. And there, unchanging, among the plants, was a small, solitary stone pagoda.

As he watched the scene disappear into the gathering darkness, he would no longer resent his hour-and-a-half commute. Nor would he mind his position at work — Administration Manager — a job with no prospects. The only prospect that interested him was the prospect over his garden.

厚子も夫の気持が判っているらしく、いつもは二言三言で引き下るのだが、この日は妙にしつこかった。宅次もいつになく尖った声で、

「マンションなんか建てたら、おれは働かないよ」

と言い返した。

指先に挾んだ煙草が落ちたのは、そのときである。

風かな、と思った。

ふっと風にもってゆかれた、そんな感じだった。

「風があるのかな」

宅次は呟いた。

「風なんかないでしょ。風があれば、洗濯もの、乾いてますよ」

厚子は縁側に出てくると、自分の人さし指をペロリと嘗め、蠟燭を立てるように立てて見せた。

「風なんかありませんよ」

九つ年下の厚子は、子供のいないせいもあるのだろう、年に似合わぬいたずらっぽいしぐさをすることがある。西瓜の種子みたいに小さいが黒光りする目が、自分の趣向を面白がって躍っているのを見ると、宅次は煙草のことを言い出すのが億劫になった。

Atsuko seemed to appreciate how her husband felt, and normally she let the matter drop quite quickly. But on that day she was strangely persistent. And Takuji responded with unusual irritation. 'If we build on the garden, I'm giving up work,' he said.

It was just then that the cigarette fell from his fingers.

Takuji thought it might be the wind. A breeze had suddenly lifted the cigarette from his fingers. That's what it felt like.

'*Is* there a wind?' he muttered.

'There's no wind, I'm sure,' said Atsuko. 'If there was a wind, the clothes would be dry, wouldn't they?' Coming out onto the veranda, she licked her forefinger and thrust it vertically in the air, candle-like.

'No, there's no wind at all.'

Nine years younger than Takuji, Atsuko had a mischievous, rather immature side — perhaps, in part, because she had no children. Her eyes were small, bright and black, like watermelon seeds. Takuji watched them dance with delight, his wife revelling in her little performance. He could no longer be bothered to mention the cigarette.

中年。手足のしびれ感。何という薬の広告だったか、こんな文句があったと思いながら、沓脱の石の上で細い煙を上げている煙草を拾った。手袋をはめたまま物を摑むような厚ぼったい感じがすこし気になった。

あとから考えれば、これが最初の前触れだった。

この何日あとだったか、仕事中不意に目の前にいる次長の名前が思い出せなくなった。その日だったか次の日か、つきあいで酒を飲み、送りのタクシーで帰ったとき、車から降りたとたんに、糸の切れた操り人形のようにくたくたとなり、地面に坐り込んでしまった。運転手に助け起されてすぐに直ったが、あれも前兆だったのである。

指先の煙草を落してから一週間目に、宅次は起きぬけに朝刊を取りにゆき、茶の間へもどったところで、障子の桟につかまりながら、わからなくなった。

脳卒中の発作だった。

頭のなかで地虫が鳴いている。

倒れてからひと月になるが、地虫は宅次の頭の、ちょうど首のうしろあたりで、じじ、じじ、と思い出したように鳴いていた。

It had landed on a stepping stone down below the veranda. There it lay, sending up a thin plume of smoke. As he picked it up, Takuji recalled the words of a medicine advertisement: 'Middle-aged? Numb hands? Numb feet?' It felt as though he were holding the cigarette through a glove. It was a strange sensation.

Looking back, this was the first sign of what was to come.

A few days later at work, he suddenly found he could not remember the name of his boss, who was standing just in front of him. It was either that day or the next that he went drinking with some colleagues and took a taxi home. When he climbed out of the car he lost all coordination in his limbs and slumped to the ground like a puppet with its strings cut. The taxi driver helped him up, and he soon recovered. But this had been another sign.

A week after he dropped the cigarette, he got up in the morning and went to fetch the newspaper from the letter box. Coming back, he clutched at the frame of the sliding door and collapsed.

He had had a stroke.

A grub was fidgeting in his head.

In the month since his stroke the grub had been fidgeting and squeaking at the back of his neck. *ji-ji,* it went, *ji-ji,* like a persistent, niggling memory.

意識が薄れたのは、ほんの一時間ほどだったが、それでも右半身に軽い麻痺が残った。杖にすがればどうにか歩けるが、右手はまだ箸が覚束なかった。

厚子が鼻唄を歌っている。

宅次が倒れてから、厚子はよく鼻唄を歌うようになった。病気は大したことないのよ。そのうち、きっとよくなるわよ。あたし、決して悲観なんかしていないわよ。そういう代りに鼻唄を歌っているように見えた。

もともと、こまめなたちだったが、宅次が会社を休職して、寝たり起きたりになると、厚子は前にも増して、よく体を動かした。坐っているときは、豆の莢をむいたりレースを編んだり何かしら手を動かしていた。することがない時でも、目玉だけはいつも動いていた。

玄関に人の来た気配がする。車のセールスマンらしい。主人が倒れたので車どころじゃないのよ、と言うかなと耳をすますと、

「ごめんなさいね。うちの主人、車のほうなの」

歌うような厚子の声が聞えた。

He had recovered full consciousness about an hour after the stroke, but there was still some paralysis on the right side of his body. He could just about manage a walking stick, but chopsticks were much too difficult.

Atsuko was humming. She had been humming a lot since his stroke. She might have said, 'It's not that serious', or, 'You'll be fine in no time', or, 'I'm not at all pessimistic'. But she didn't. Instead, it seemed, she hummed.

She was a busily attentive person anyway, but now that Takuji was in the house all day as an invalid, she seemed in almost constant motion. When seated, her hands were always moving — shelling peas, sewing lace. If she had nothing in particular to do, her eyes would dart around the room.

Someone was at the door. A car salesman. Takuji listened. He expected Atsuko to say something like, 'My husband's ill. We really can't think about cars now.' But no.

'Oh, I'm sorry. My husband's in the car trade himself,' she said in a sing-song voice.

そうだ。厚子はいつもこのやりかただった。

化粧品のセールスだと、主人は化粧品関係になったし、百科辞典がくると出版関係になった。新婚の頃、毛布を売りにきた押売りを、

「うちの主人、繊維関係なのよ」

歌うような口振りで追い払い、奥にいた宅次を振り返って、目だけで笑ってみせた。面白い女と一緒になった、一生退屈しないだろうと宅次は思ったが、その通りだった。

嘘も方便という程度の他愛ない嘘をつくとき、歌うような声になるのを一緒に面白がっている分には、気働きはあるし情も濃い。宅次には過ぎた女房といえるだろう。その嘘にしても、つまりは宅次のためうちのため役に立つ頓智の領分だった。

顔の幅だけ襖があいて、厚子が顔を出した。

二十年前と同じ笑い顔だった。指でつまんだような小さな鼻は、笑うと上を向いた。それでなくても離れている目は、ますます離れて、おどけてみえた。何かに似ている、と思ったが、思い出せなかった。病気のせいか、脳味噌のほうも半分分厚い半透明のビニールをかぶったようで焦れったくなる。

こういうとき、頭のなかの地虫は、じじ、じじ、と鳴くのである。

Of course. That's what she always did. With cosmetics salesmen, her husband was in cosmetics. With encyclopaedia people, he was in publishing. Soon after they married, a man had come to sell blankets.

'Actually, my husband's in the textile business himself,' she had said.

Having got rid of the salesman, she had turned back towards Takuji, her eyes laughing. I'll never be bored with a woman like this, he had thought. And he was right.

He enjoyed the sing-song tone of these little white lies. They seemed sensible and kind. They showed how quick-witted she was. And this wit was employed to protect Takuji, to protect their home. He did not deserve such a wonderful wife.

The sliding screen opened — just wide enough for Atsuko to show her face. Her smile was the same as twenty years before. It lifted her small, pinched nose, making her eyes seem still wider apart than usual. It was a comical sight. It reminded Takuji of something, but he couldn't remember what. This irritated him, as if his brain was inside an opaque plastic bag.

It was at times like these that the grub in his head began to fidget and squeak: *ji-ji, ji-ji*.

厚子は赤いクリーム・ソーダを飲んでいる。いい年をして、ストローをぶくぶく吹くものだから、アイスクリームのまざった赤く色のついたソーダ水は、白いあぶくが立っている。

厚子のくわえているストローは、縦にひび割れていたらしい。割れ目から、赤いソーダ水が溢れてきた。

「よせ。吸うのはよせ」

今度血管から血が溢れたら、おれは一巻の終りだ。

叫ぼうとするのだが声が出ない、というところで揺り起された。

夢かうつつか。つなぎ目がはっきりしなくなっている。新婚の頃、デパートの食堂で、ソーダ水を飲んでいて、厚子のストローがひび割れて、いきなりソーダ水があふれてきたことがあったような気がするが、色は赤だったか青だったのか。

厚子は、いつの間に着替えたのか、よそゆきの着物を着て、布団のすぐ横に坐っていた。

「この間から、話してたあれ、出かけて来ますね」

あれと言われても、とっさには思い当らない。

高校のときの先生が、勲章をもらった。同窓会でお祝いを上げることになったので幹事だけでデパートへ下見にゆくというのだが、そんなはなしは初耳のような気がする。

Atsuko was drinking a red ice-cream soda. Like a child, she blew down her straw into the glass, sending white bubbles up to the surface.

As she sucked and blew, the red liquid began to leak through a split in the side of the straw.

'Stop it! Stop sucking!'

The blood will come out of my veins. That'll be the end! He tried to shout, but he couldn't. Then he was shaken awake.

Was that a dream? Or reality? The distinction was blurred. He thought he could remember drinking ice-cream sodas in a shop restaurant when they were first married. Atsuko's straw had split and the soda had leaked out. But he could not remember if the liquid was red or blue.

Atsuko had changed into a smart kimono. She knelt beside Takuji's futon.

'You know that thing I was talking about? I've got to go out and get it done.'

He couldn't immediately remember what 'that thing' was.

Her old high-school teacher had received an official honour and the alumni were to buy him a congratulatory gift. The committee were going out to the shops to look for something.

Takuji didn't remember hearing about that before.

「お三時はメロン冷えてるけど、帰ってからでいいでしょ」

　厚子は、着やせのするたちだが、脚の太いのを気にして、気の張る外出はいつも和服である。それはいいのだが、相手によって衿元が二段階に分かれていることに、宅次は前から気がついていた。

　宅次や親戚の女たちと出かけるときは、格別胸元を取りつくろうことをしないが、よく見られたいときは、胸をぐっと押上げるような着付けをする。

　細い夏蜜柑の木に、よく生ったものだと思うほど重たそうな夏蜜柑が実っているのがある。結婚した当座の厚子はそんな風だった。さすがに四十を越して夏蜜柑も幾分小さめになったようだが、ここ一番というときになると、厚子は上に持ち上げて、昔の夏蜜柑にするのである。

　これから逢う相手は女ではないような気もするが、この病気の特徴は、ひがみっぽくなることだと書いてあった。気持を鎮めなくてはいけない。腹を立てないのが一番の薬と主治医の竹沢に言われている。

　厚子のおろしたての白足袋が、弾むように縁側を小走りにゆくのを見ると、気がつかないうちに、おい、と呼びとめていた。

'There's some chilled melon for a snack this afternoon. But let's wait till I get back, shall we?'

Atsuko looked slim in most clothes, but she was worried by her stubby legs and so usually wore a kimono for any kind of outing. That was fine. But Takuji had noticed some time ago that the way she wore her kimono would vary according to whom she was going to see. When going out with Takuji or female relatives, she would wear her kimono in a normal way; but when she wanted to look attractive, she would arrange the kimono so as to lift her bust.

At the time of their marriage, Atsuko's figure had been perfect — a slender citrus tree with full, heavy fruit. Of course, since the age of forty the fruit had shrunk somewhat, but when occasion called she would push it up and restore its plumpness.

Takuji thought she might be going to meet a man. But he had read that people with his condition were prone to jealousy. He must relax. According to Dr Takezawa, the best medicine was to avoid anger.

He saw her new white kimono socks tripping happily along the veranda.

'Oi,' he called involuntarily.

She stopped and turned.

「なんじゃ」

　わざと時代劇のことば使いで、ひょいとおどけて振り向いた厚子を見て、宅次は、あ、と声を立てそうになった。

　なにかに似ていると思ったのは、かわうそだった。

　デパートの屋上でかわうそを見たのは、何年前のことだったか。

　昼休みにぶらりとのぞいた、子供のための小動物を集めたコーナーのプールに、二頭のかわうそがふざけていた。

　どちらが牡でどちらが牝かわからなかったが、二頭ともじっとしているということがなかった。水に浮かんだ木の葉を魚にでも見たてているのか、わざと物々しく様子をつくってぶつかってゆく。

　そうかと思うと、ポカンとした顔をして浮いている。ポカンとしている癖に、左右に離れた黒い小さな目は、油断なく動いているらしく、硬貨をじゃらつかせて餌の泥鰌入れに近寄る気配を見せると、二頭は先を争って、泥鰌の落ちてくる筒の下で、人間の手のような前肢をすり合せ、キイキイとにぎやかに騒ぎ立て催促する。

　厚かましいが憎めない。ずるそうだが目の放せない愛嬌があった。

　ひとりでに体がはしゃいでしまい、生きて動いていることが面白くて嬉しくてたまらないというところは、厚子と同じだ。

'What is it, my lord?' she said, in the manner of a samurai drama, her face suddenly comical.

Takuji almost gasped. He remembered what it was that she resembled — an otter.

How long was it since he saw those otters? He had walked out onto the roof terrace of a department store one lunch hour and found a children's mini zoo. Among the collection of small animals was a pair of otters playing in a pool — one was male, one female, but he couldn't tell which was which. Neither was still, not even for a moment. Seeing a leaf in the pool, they made a great show of plunging towards it, as though it were a fish. The next moment, they were floating nonchalantly on the surface, but their small, black, widely spaced eyes were still moving, constantly alert. When Takuji stepped towards the feed bin, jangling some change, the otters reacted immediately, jostling to be first at the base of the chute. They clamoured for fish, shrieking and rubbing together their hand-like paws.

He liked these cheeky creatures. They were sly, of course, but they were captivating. He could not take his eyes off them. Their joy in life and movement, the way their bodies frisked and cavorted: they were just like Atsuko.

一軒おいて隣りから、火が出たことがある。

幸い大事には到らなかったが、

「火事ですよお。火事ですよお」

寝巻で空のバケツを叩き、隣り近所を起して廻っていた厚子は、そばで見ていて気がひけるほど楽しそうに見えた。

宅次の父の葬式のときもそうだった。

厚子は新調の喪服を着て、涙をこぼすというかたちではしゃいでいた。ほうっておくと、泣きながら、笑い出しそうな気がして、宅次は、

「おだつな」

とたしなめるところだった。

おだつ、というのは、宅次の田舎の仙台あたりで使うことばで、調子づく、といった意味である。

右手でふたつの胡桃を廻しながら、宅次は庭を見ていた。胡桃は、右手の麻痺の恢復にいいと聞いて、厚子が買ってきたものである。

左手で廻すと、ふたつの胡桃はカスタネットのような冴えた音を立ててぶつかるが、右手でやると、鈍い濁った病気の音がした。

There was once a fire in the house next door but one. Luckily, it was not serious, but that did not prevent Atsuko walking around the neighbourhood in her nightclothes, waking everybody up. 'Fire! Fire!' she shouted, hitting an empty bucket with a stick. Her enjoyment in the drama was so evident that Takuji felt uncomfortable watching her.

It was the same at his father's funeral.

Dressed in new mourning clothes, Atsuko seemed to take delight in her tears. Takuji felt that if he didn't do something, laughter might come bursting through.

'*Odatsuna*!' he had been about to say. Cut it out! His family was from northern Japan and it was a dialect expression that hovered on his lips.

Takuji was looking at the garden, trying to rotate two walnuts in his right hand. Atsuko had bought them, hearing this exercise might speed his recovery. He could manipulate the walnuts well with his left hand, making a clear sound, like a castanet. But in his right hand the sound was dull, muffled, ill.

宅次は、小机の前に坐って、ペンを握ってみた。足がしびれて立てないときのもどかしさ、熱い新湯に入ったときの刺すような痛みが妙な具合にまざって、自分の手ではなかった。いつになったら字が書けるのか。宅次は先のことは考えまいと思っている。考え出すと、首すじのうしろで、地虫がじじ、じじ、と鳴きはじめる。

ひとりで眺める庭は慰めにならなかった。

志を得ない勤めの鬱憤を胸に仕舞って、うしろに厚子がいてなんやかやと半畳を入れながら眺めるから、よかったのである。

学校の休み時間と同じであろう。

勉強のあい間に、五分かそこらだから、仲間がいるからボール遊びも面白いのだ。一日中遊んでよろしいといわれ、ボールをあてがわれても、たったひとりでは、ただのゴムの球体に過ぎない。

厚子を気ぜわしいと思うこともないではないが、やはり、このうちにかわうそは一頭いたほうがいい。

電話が鳴った。

畳をいざって、受話器をとった。左手でつかみ左の耳にあてるしぐさがやっと身についてきた。以前は右で聞いていたのだが、いま右の耳には目に見えない羽虫が飛んでいることがある。

He sat at a small desk and tried picking up a pen. Was that really his hand? The appearance and the sensation were quite at odds with each other. He felt a strange combination of the irritation one feels when unable to stand up because of a numb leg, and the sharp pain when getting into a very hot bath. But the familiar feeling of holding a pen was completely absent. When would he be able to write again? But he tried not to think about the future. If he did, the grub would start to fidget and squeak at the back of his neck: *ji-ji, ji-ji.*

There was no consolation in looking at the garden when he was alone. The enjoyment came when, pent up with the frustration of his dead-end job, he had Atsuko behind him, teasing him. It was like breaktime at school. When you have five minutes or so away from your desk, playing ball is fun because others are there. But if you are given the whole day and you are on your own, then the ball is just a spherical piece of rubber. Despite her restlessness, the house was better for the presence of his otter-like wife.

The telephone rang.

Takuji crawled across the floor to pick up the receiver. At last, he was used to taking it in his left hand and putting it to his left ear. Before his stroke, he had always listened with his right ear, but now that was home to a buzzing insect.

電話の声は今里だった。

大学時代からの友達で、かれこれ四十年のつきあいになる。宅次が倒れたとき、厚子に一番先に電話をかけさせたのも今里だった。

「言いたいことあったら、おれ、代りに言ってやるぞ」

もともと時候の挨拶などするつきあいではないが、それにしても唐突だった。

「お前、本当にいいのか」

ひと呼吸あって、

「それだけは、嫌だっていってたからさ。本当にいいのかと思ってね。まあ、こうなったら、仕方ないよなあ」

一体、なんのはなしだと問いつめると、今度は今里がうろたえた。

「お前、知らないのか」

厚子の発案で、宅次の今後のことを相談する集りにこれから出かけるところだという。メンバーは、次長の坪井、マキノ不動産と近所の銀行の支店長代理、主治医の竹沢、それに今里だという。

厚子は庭をつぶしてマンションを建て、借入れした銀行に管理してもらって、若手行員たちの社宅にしたいと考えているらしい。

The call was from Imazato, an old university friend he had known for forty years. Imazato was the first person Takuji had asked Atsuko to contact after his stroke.

'If there's anything you want said, I'll say it for you.'

Of course, these old friends never stood on ceremony, but even so, Imazato's first words seemed abrupt.

'Is it really okay?' Imazato continued.

He paused. 'I mean you said you definitely didn't want it to happen, so I wondered... But maybe with things as they are, it can't be helped.'

Takuji had to ask Imazato what he was talking about.

'You don't know?' said Imazato, the confusion now his.

He explained that Atsuko had invited him to a meeting that afternoon to discuss Takuji's future. The participants were to be Tsuboi — Takuji's boss — the estate agent, the deputy manager of the local bank, Dr Takezawa, Imazato and Atsuko. Atsuko was proposing to build the apartment block over the garden and have it managed by the bank, which would provide a loan. It would be used as accommodation for young bank staff.

宅次は、頭のなかが、ふくれ上ってゆくのが判った。五人の男たちに囲まれている厚子が見えて来た。

高く盛り上げた夏蜜柑の胸を突き出し、黒光りする目を躍らせて、健気な妻の役を生き生きと演じているに違いない。

それにしても五人は多過ぎる。次長の坪井が何の役に立つというのだ。

学生時代に見た一枚の絵が不意に浮かんで来た。

あれは梅原だったか劉生だったか。白く濁ったビニール袋をかぶった脳味噌では思い出せないが、構図は覚えている。

かなり大きい油絵で、画面いっぱいに旧式の牛乳瓶、花、茶碗、ミルクポット、食べかけの果物、パンの切れっぱし、首をしめられてぐったりした鳥が、卓上せましとならんでいた。

題は「獺祭図」である。

宅次は、この字が読めず意味も判らなかった。

うちに帰り辞書をひいて、やっとわかったのだが、これはかわうそのお祭りだという。

かわうそは、いたずら好きである。食べるためでなく、ただ獲物をとる面白さだけで沢山の魚を殺すことがある。

Takuji felt himself losing his composure. He pictured Atsuko surrounded by the five men, throwing herself into the role of devoted wife, her bust pushed out, her black eyes dancing. Five was too many. What on earth was Tsuboi supposed to be doing there? Takuji suddenly remembered a painting he had seen when he was a student.

It may have been by Umehara. Or perhaps Ryusei. He could not decipher the name through the plastic bag which covered his brain. But he could recall the picture itself. It was a large oil painting — the canvas was crowded with old-fashioned milk bottles, flowers, bowls, a milk jug, half-eaten fruit, pieces of bread, a bird with its neck wrung, all crammed onto a table.

The title was 獺祭図, but he had been uncertain as to how to read the characters. Looking the word up in a dictionary at home he discovered that it was read *Dassaizu,* meaning 'The Otters' Carnival'. Otters are wanton in their destructiveness: they sometimes kill more fish than they can possibly eat, and lay them out on display. That kind of display is sometimes called an otters' carnival.

殺した魚をならべて、たのしむ習性があるというので、数多くのものをならべて見せることを獺祭図というらしい。

火事も葬式も、夫の病気も、厚子にとっては、体のはしゃぐお祭りなのである。

宅次は、牛乳瓶のうしろで死んでいる鳥が見えて来た。鳥は目をあいて死んでいたが、あの子は目をつぶっていた。

星江は、三つで死んだ宅次のひとり娘だった。

朝、出がけに、宅次は星江のおでこに自分の額をくっつけ、熱があるぞ、竹沢先生に往診を頼めよ、と声をかけて出張に出かけた。三日後、出張先に電話がかかり、急性肺炎で危篤だという。仕事もそこそこに帰京した時、星江の顔には白い布がかかっていた。

厚子は、あの日竹沢医院に電話をしたが、取次の手違いで往診が次の日になったと泣いていた。竹沢医師も、新入りの見習い看護婦の手落ちということで、宅次に頭を下げた。宅次の父が、人を責めても死んだ人間は帰らないよ、と間に入り、ことを納めたのである。

死児の齢をかぞえながら、忘れるともなく忘れていた頃、宅次は駅で、結婚のため田舎へ帰るその看護婦に逢った。

ためらいながら、宅次の横に立ち、

「黙って帰るつもりだったんですけど」

The fire, the funeral and her husband's illness — they had all been carnivals for Atsuko, occasions for her to display, to cavort.

Takuji pictured the dead bird that lay behind a milk bottle in the painting. Its eyes were open. The child's eyes were shut. His only child, Hoshie. She died when she was three.

Just before he left the house that morning, he had laid his forehead against hers.

'Call Dr Takezawa,' he had said to Atsuko. 'She's got a fever.'

And then he left for a business trip. While still away, three days later, he received a telephone call. Hoshie was critically ill with pneumonia. He returned to Tokyo immediately, but by the time he got home, there was a white cloth over his daughter's face.

Atsuko explained through her tears how she had telephoned Dr Takezawa, but that the message she had left had not been passed on. The doctor had not come until the next day. The doctor apologised to Takuji for what had been a mistake by a trainee nurse. Takuji's father intervened: there was no point in blaming anyone; that wouldn't bring Hoshie back.

Takuji never forgot his daughter. He imagined her growing up, as the years went by. Yet at the same time, the memory grew less sharp. Then one day, at the station, he met the nurse. She was leaving to get married in her home town. She stood beside him hesitantly.

'I wasn't going to say anything,' she mumbled.

口ごもるオールドミス、といった感じの女を、はじめは誰か判らなかった。

「あの日、電話はなかったんですよ」

厚子が往診をたのんだのは次の日だったという。前の日、厚子はクラス会だった。

宅次は、その夜、したたかに酒をのんだ。

玄関のガラス戸をあけるなり、厚子の頬を思い切り殴ってやる。そう思って帰ってきた。

宅次は殴らなかった。

なぜだったのか。思い出そうとすると、頭のうしろが、じじ、じじと鳴る。この女を殴らないほうがいい、とどこかで思ったから、黙って玄関へ入り、酒の勢いで眠ったのだろう。

庭にうすい墨がかかってきた。松も楓も五輪も、もうどっちでもよかった。

この時間が一番頭が重たくなる。いずれはみんな無くなって、モルタルの安手な四角い家が立ちふさがるのだ。

Takuji didn't recognise her at first — an unfamiliar woman in her late twenties.

'Nobody telephoned,' she continued. 'Nobody telephoned that day.'

It had been the following day that Atsuko telephoned the doctor. The day Takuji left for his business trip, Atsuko was at a class reunion.

That evening, Takuji drank heavily. On his way home, he imagined himself opening the door and punching Atsuko's face.

But he did not punch her.

He tried to remember why, but the grub began to fidget and squeak: *ji-ji, ji-ji.* For some reason, he must have felt it was better not to hit this woman. And so he went in quietly through the entrance hall, and when he lay down the alcohol carried him off to sleep.

Shades of charcoal began to gather over the garden. It was becoming difficult to distinguish the pines, the maples, the stone pagoda — and Takuji no longer cared. This was the time of day his head felt heaviest. Before long, the whole garden would disappear under a cheap, square, mortar-clad block.

厚子の声が聞えてきた。

宅次の具合をたずねる隣りの奥さんに、何かしゃべっている。歌うような声で、明日のお天気を話すように宅次の血圧のはなしをしている。

宅次は立ち上った。

障子につかまりながら、台所へゆき、気がついたら庖丁を握っていた。刺したいのは自分の胸なのか、厚子の夏蜜柑の胸なのか判らなかった。

「凄いじゃないの」

厚子だった。

「庖丁持てるようになったのねえ。もう一息だわ」

屈託のない声だった。左右に離れた西瓜の種子みたいな、黒い小さな目が躍っていた。

「メロン、食べようと思ってさ」

宅次は、庖丁を流しに落すように置くと、ぎくしゃくした足どりで、縁側のほうへ歩いていった。首のうしろで地虫がさわいでいる。

「メロンねえ、銀行からのと、マキノからのと、どっちにします」

返事は出来なかった。

写真機のシャッターがおりるように、庭が急に闇になった。

He heard Atsuko's voice. The woman next door had asked after him and Atsuko was talking about his blood pressure. In her sing-song voice she sounded as though she were discussing the weather forecast.

Takuji stood up.

Clutching the paper screen, he made his way to the kitchen. Before he noticed quite what he was doing, he had picked up a knife. Was it to stab himself or Atsuko? He hardly knew.

'That's wonderful!' said Atsuko, coming into the kitchen. 'Look at you! You can hold a knife! Well, we haven't got far to go now, have we?'

Her voice was carefree. Her widely spaced, black, seed-like eyes were dancing.

'I was going to have some melon,' Takuji said, putting — or rather dropping — the knife into the sink. He walked unsteadily towards the veranda. The grub was growing restless.

'Oh yes, melon!' said Atsuko. 'Shall we have the one the bank gave us — or the one from the estate agent?'

Takuji could make no reply.

Darkness had come over the garden suddenly, like the closing of a camera's shutter.

黒田夏子　Natsuko Kuroda

1937年東京生まれ。2013年「***ab*** さんご」で芥川賞受賞。受賞にいたるまでは、主に校正の仕事をしてきたが、常に自分自身の作品を書き続けてきた。「***ab*** さんご（***ab*** Sango）」の抄訳（Words without Borders）、「道の声（The Voice on the Road）」（Two Lines Journal）を英語で読むことができる。「毬」は1963年に、読売短編小説賞を受賞している。「毬」の英訳は、2014年ジョン・ドライデン翻訳コンクールの奨励賞受賞作に基づく。

Natsuko Kuroda was born in Tokyo in 1937. She won the Akutagawa Prize in 2013 for '***ab*** Sango'. Since then work translated into English includes an extract from '***ab*** Sango' (Words without Borders) and 'The Voice on the Road' (Two Lines Journal). Before 2013 she had spent much of her career as a proof reader, but has always been an active writer. 'Mari' ('Ball') won the Yomiuri Newspaper Short Story Prize in 1963. The translation is based on a version commended in the 2014 John Dryden Translation Competition.

毬

Ball

黒田夏子

Natsuko Kuroda

毬は黒光りして硬く、タミエの掌のくぼみにきっちり嵌りに昇って来た。何度だって昇って来た。強く打ちつければ強く、毬は撥ね上がってタミエの掌に戻った。

タミエは、みんなと毬で遊ぶとすればどうしてもしなければならないあれこれの芸当に関しては、そのうちの一番易しいのでさえ、なんとも見ていられないほど下手で、というより、滅多にできたことなんかないのであった。でも、ただ突いているというだけならいくらでも続く。毬を突く、ということはこういうことなんだとタミエは一人で合点し、そして大抵一人で突いた。街並から奥まった庭の広い邸の、常には開けられることのない表門の甃などで。タミエの家だったらその門構えの中に、そっくり一軒建ったろう。白っぽく、広々と閑かで、毬の音は世界中を充たすように響く。その遠い木霊を聴きながら、鈍く光る毬の上下するのに見入っていると、気が遠くなりそうな、続けることが哀しく、続けないことはなお哀しく、いたたまれない快と不快のごちゃまぜに縛りつけられ、そんな時ふと吹き通る風に花の匂いがしたりすると、タミエは怒ったように毬を叩きつけた。それでも毬は光って丸く硬く、タミエの掌のくぼみにちょうどいい大きさで忠実に返った。

The hard, black, shiny ball rose sweetly into the hollow of Tamie's palm. Up it came, time and again. The harder she threw it down, the harder it came bouncing back up into her palm.

Tamie was no good at all those tricks you had to perform when playing with the others. It was painful to watch her doing even the simplest; in fact, she'd hardly ever managed to *do* any of them. But when it came to just bouncing, she was fine. She could keep going as long as she liked. This is how you bounce, she said to herself, nodding. Normally, she bounced on her own. She often used the area of paving by the front gate of a big house near by. The house stood in a large garden, well away from the busy streets. Its gateway, under which you could have fitted Tamie's own house in its entirety, was seldom opened. In this broad, white, quiet space the sound of the ball seemed to fill the world. Tamie listened to its distant echo and watched intently as the dark, dimly shining ball moved up and down. She felt herself drifting away. She was bound up in an unbearable jumble of pleasure and pain: it was sad to continue, but sadder still to stop. And if, just then, the smell of flowers, say, wafted towards her on the wind, she would fling the ball down as though in anger. But even then, the hard, round, shining ball would come faithfully back again, snug into her palm.

タミエは時々小声で歌った。でたらめに。山鳩が、寝呆けた声で啼いたので、どこにいるかと探していたら、山鳩いなくて百合の花、藪の中には百合の花、大きな大きな百合の花………。

タミエの友だちの歌う、本当の毬唄はこういうのだ――一リットラ、一コーシ、シラホケキョーノ、タカチホヨ、ジョーテンカ。

タミエには何の事だかさっぱりわからない。でもみんなとてもよくわかっているような顔をしているから訊いてみるわけにもいかない。終りのところがジョーテンカではなくてリョーテンカだと云い張ったサアちゃんと松ちゃんの大喧嘩の時には、タミエさえも意見を求められた。普段はタミエなんかどうせものの数には入らないのだが、リョーテンカの支持者があんまり少なかったものだからサアちゃんは躍起になって、とうとうタミエにまで持ち掛けたのだ。ねえ、タミちゃんもそう思うでしょう？　ジョーテンカなんて変よ。リョーテンカよ。ね、絶対よね。もちろんタミエはサアちゃんの

Sometimes she sang quietly to herself, as she bounced the ball. She sang complete nonsense.

> A pigeon cooed in a sleepy voice
> I looked for him, but he wasn't there
> A lily grew in a great thick bush,
> Tall it grew where the pigeon cooed

The proper ball song that Tamie's friends sang went like this:

> One *rittora,* One *ko-shi,*
> *Shira hokekyo-no, Taka chiho yo,*
> *Jo-tenka*

Tamie didn't have the faintest idea what this meant. But everybody else looked as though they understood perfectly, so she couldn't very well ask. There was once a big argument between Mat-chan and Saa-chan, after Saa-chan claimed the last line was not '*jo-tenka*' at all, but '*ryo-tenka*'. Even Tamie was asked for her opinion. Normally, nobody took any account of her, but '*ryo-tenka*' had so few supporters that Saa-chan became desperate and eventually approached her.

'*Jo-tenka* sounds odd, doesn't it? Tami-chan,' she said. 'It's *ryo-tenka,* isn't it? You agree with me, don't you? It's obvious!'

勢いにたじたじとなって逆わずにいたものの、どっちみち全然わからないし、何語だかも定かでない。ホケキョーとかタカチホとかいうところはどうやら日本語のようでもあるが、それだって勝手にそう聞き取った者のこじつけた発音かもしれない。ともかくわかっていることは、これが一リットラから十リットラまで続いて、次には一リットランラン、一コーシッシ、シラホケキョーノッノ、タカチホヨッヨ、ジョーテンカ。という風になって、つまり、節のくぎり目でする曲突きを、二度ずつ続けてやるのを又十リットランランまでやって、その又次は左手で一リットラから……という工合の、タミエには限りもなく長く思われる遊びの順序と、それから、一コーシの「コー」というところでひどく高い音になるのでタミエは声を出すのをやめる、ということである。別にタミエの声帯が、並の女の子と違っているわけはないのだが、どうも高すぎる節まわしだと感じると、タミエは声を止めてしまうのである。全体を低い調子で歌っていたって、やっぱり「コー」というところは声を出さない。順番を待っている者はみんな歌っているので、タミエ一人がいつもそこで、口だけその形にして声を出していないという事情は誰にも正確には知れないのだが、それでもなんとなく

Of course, Tamie, quailing at Saa-chan's forceful manner, didn't disagree, but the truth was she had no idea — she couldn't even say what language it was. Parts like *hokekyo* and *taka chiho* certainly sounded as though they might be Japanese, but that could just have been because someone had decided to hear them like that, giving them Japanese pronunciation.

What Tamie *did* know was the order of this seemingly endless game, which, having gone from *one rittora* to *ten rittora,* then started again, with the last syllable of each phrase doubled to allow a repeat of the critical movements.

*One rittora*nran *One ko-shi*sshi
*Shira hokekyo-no*nno *Taka chiho yo*yyo
Jo-tenka

And then, once they had gone from *one rittoranran* to *ten rittoranran,* they went back again to *one rittora,* and repeated the whole process, this time bouncing the ball left-handed.

She also knew that the *ko-* in *ko-shi* was a terribly high-pitched sound that she would not sing. It wasn't that her vocal cords were any different from those of other girls; it was just that when she felt the pitch was too high, she would stop. She wouldn't utter *ko-,* even if the song was being sung in a lower pitch than normal. Everybody sang together while they were waiting for their turn, so nobody could know for certain that

タミエがいんちきをしているという印象は漂うのである。そういう感じのために、タミエは決して信用されなかった。これは嘘、それはいんちきだと指摘できないからこそ、うろんさはいよいよ確かなのである。

一リットラは右脚を上げて毬をまたぐ。二リットラは右脚の外側から右手を差し入れて突く。三リットラは爪先で突く。四リットラは右膝で軽く上へ突き上げる。五リットラは、足は地面から離さないまま、右脚の膝を巧みに曲げて、毬を前から後へくぐらす。六リットラはそれを左脚で。七リットラは再び右側の、今度は後から前へ。八リットラはそれを左側で。九リットラは両足を上げて毬の上を横へ跳び越す。十リットラは高く弾ませておく間に、自分がその場でくるりとまわる。そこまで行くとお続けというのをやる。それまでの技巧を一度ずつ並べるのだ。もちろんタミエはそんなところまでなんか行ったことはない。一番進めた時でも五リットラで日が暮れる。なぜならタミエは一度も五リットラの突き方に成功した例しがないのだから、そこまで来ればもう、何度でもその失敗を繰返しているほかないのである。

Tamie was simply mouthing *ko-*, but nevertheless, there was a general feeling that somehow she was cheating. And so she wasn't trusted at all. The very fact that they couldn't specify that *this* was a lie, or *that* was cheating only served to render her still more suspicious.

At *one rittora,* you lifted your right leg over the ball as it bounced. At *two rittora,* you put your right hand under your right leg and bounced the ball there. At *three rittora,* you bounced the ball with the tips of your toes. At *four rittora,* you bounced the ball lightly on your right knee. At *five,* keeping both feet on the ground, you carefully bent your right knee and bounced the ball from front to back through the gap between your legs. At *six,* you did the same, bending the left leg. At *seven,* you bent your right leg again, but this time bounced the ball from back to front. At *eight,* you did the same thing with your left leg. At *nine,* you jumped sideways over the bouncing ball. At *ten,* you bounced the ball high up in the air and spun around on the spot before it came down.

If you got that far, you'd do a *straight,* performing each of the key moves once again in quick succession. Of course, Tamie had never reached that stage. The furthest she'd ever got was *five rittora.* She'd never managed the *five-rittora* bounce; every time she got there she ended up just repeating the same errors.

みんなは大抵、一気にオツヅケ位まで行ってしまって疲れて来て手許が狂って番が変わる。だから遊び始める前に、十リットラランランの時は毬が二つ弾んでもいいことにしようとか、左手の十リットラは廻るのも左廻りね、などと、タミエには全く無縁な掟を取り決める。オノバシナシ、というのもタミエにだけは免除された。タミエにだけ規則が緩やかだということはつまりタミエが競争相手として一人前でないことに誰も異議がないからである。こういう恩典の保持者はオミソと呼ばれる。味噌っ滓の略である。お延ばしとは、曲突きをする前の弾みが適当でなかったり、運悪く石に当って方向が外れたりした時に、二つ三つ普通の突き方でつなぐことであるが、タミエの足はなかなか持ち上がらなくて二つ三つどころではなく、みんなは、トオオオ……とかコオオオ……とか長いこと延ばして、息も詰まりそうになって、やっとラとかシとか云えるのだった。気短かな仲間のいる時は、タミちゃんいい加減にしてよ、と叱られたし、いくらオノバシアリだって、十以上は差し止めようとかいうことになるのであるが、実際のところタミエが突いている時間といったら極く僅かで、一リットオオオ……ラ、でもう駄目になって番を譲るのだから、そこで十延ばそうが二十延ばそうが、一気にオツヅケやランランまで行ってしまうような連中が待ち遠しがる程のこともないのである。

Everybody else would normally get to a *straight* in one go, and after that they'd tend to get a bit tired, fumble the ball and forfeit their turn. So before playing, they'd say things like, 'You can bounce twice in *ten rittoranran*', or, 'At left-handed *ten rittora* you spin left as well' — making up rules that would never affect Tamie in the slightest.

Tamie was the only girl to be exempted from *No Extension*. The rule was relaxed for her alone because nobody regarded her as real competition. Recipients of such special treatment were called *dreggies*. An *extension* was when, if you made a mistake prior to a key move, or if the ball hit a stone, you could bounce the ball an extra two or three times to regain control. But Tamie was slow at lifting her feet and so it always took her longer than just two or three bounces to get back on track. Meanwhile, the others would be drawing out the particular syllable they had reached in the song, *to-o-o-o—*, for example, or *ko-o-o-o—*, and would barely have enough breath left to utter the following *ra* or *shi*. Sometimes a girl would get cross: 'For goodness' sake, Tami!' she'd say, and then, turning to the others, 'An extension can't go on for ever! Let's limit the number of bounces to ten.' Actually, Tamie never spent long bouncing the ball in total; she'd be on *one ritto-o-o-o—ra*, make a hash of it and forfeit her turn. So whether she bounced ten or even twenty times, the others had no reason to get impatient; *they* would all keep going far longer, getting to a *straight* or *ranran* without stopping.

冬うちは、お手玉の全盛だった。タミエはオテノセ、オツカミ、オハサミ位までは稀には行ったが、次のオコツリで始まる長い一続きの段階から先は、もう歌もよくはわからなくて混沌として、地平線の彼方という感じであった。お馬の乗り換えだとか乗り越しだとか、橋をどうするとか、その旅路の遥けさは幻の国といった趣である。そしてそんな技巧は一度もやってみたことがなく、順もわからない始末のタミエとしては、万一そんなところまですらすらと捗ってしまって、お馬のなんとかなどというのをやる羽目になり、どうやっていいのかまるっきりわからないようなことになってタミエが一度もそこまで行ったことがないのが露見してしまうのは困るから、どうしたってずっと初めの方でつっかえて、同じことばかりしているしかないのだ。

そんな風だから、何も熟練などを要しない遊びでさえも、タミエは決して勝たなかった。運さえ良ければ勝てるような遊びでうっかり勝ってしまってはいけないのだ。いかにもタミエの不器用無能が際立ってしまうだろう……。

Winter was the peak season for playing with small, colourful *otedama* beanbags. Tamie would very occasionally get as far as *Hand, Grip* or *Squeeze,* but when it came to the long bit starting with *Fish,* and everything after that, she didn't really know the song and felt utterly confused. It all seemed totally out of reach. *Change horses* and *Stay on* and *Bridge thingymabob* — it all felt like a distant journey to an unknown land. And since she had never once tried the moves and had no idea of the order, she didn't even want to get that far. If she had by some strange chance actually reached that stage and been forced to try one of those *Horse* whatnots, she wouldn't have had the slightest idea what to do, and everyone would know that she had never got that far before. But as it was, she invariably got stuck near the start and so simply had to keep repeating the same moves.

Even when it came to games that required no skill, Tamie would never win. She didn't want to win anything by chance — that would just put her hopeless incompetence at games involving skill into sharper focus.

たとえばパイナツプルチヨコレイトでも、タミエは必らず負けた。じゃんけんで紙で勝てばパイナツプル、鋏で勝てばチヨコレイト、石で勝てばグリコの、その字数だけ歩き、沢山の距離を進んだ者が勝である。道で、あらかじめ決めておいた所まで着いたら又逆に戻って来る、という風にするのだが、それでも日が落ちるともう互いの出した手の形が読めないほど離れてしまって、大声で自分の出したのがなんであるか叫び合うことがある。するとタミエは、勝っているのにわざと違うのを云ったりする。得にならない嘘というものが考え及ばないたちの仲間は、もちろんタミエが他の者の出した手を知った後で自分の負け手を報告する場合の真偽についてはっ疑ってみたことがないのであるが、それでもなにがなし又例のうろんさが匂って、実際はタミエがその惨敗よりも更に輪を掛けて負けるべきだったのだという気持になるのである。

毬は孤りでも突けるので、タミエはこの遊びがはやったことに感謝してよかった。タミエの毬は大きく立派ではないし、黄色いチョッキに蝶ネクタイなんかのおどけた動物の絵がついているわけでもないが、硬く張り切っていて、タミエの掌にちょうどよくて、忠実で丸くて光っていた。

She always lost at their walking version of *Rock-Paper-Scissors,* for example. Winning with *rock* gave you four paces — the number of letters in the word 'rock'; likewise a win with *paper* gave five paces and *scissors,* eight. Whoever walked farthest was the winner overall. When you got to a particular spot on the road, you turned and started back in the opposite direction, but even so, there would be quite a distance between the players, and when the sun went down it became difficult to see what shapes people were making with their hands. So everybody shouted out their choices. In these situations, Tamie would wait for everybody else to shout, and then, if she had actually won, she would sometimes change her choice to make it seem as though she'd lost. None of the others would have imagined it possible to tell a lie against one's own interest, so they never doubted the truth of what she said. But again, there seemed to be something suspicious in her behaviour, so even when Tamie had been utterly trounced, the others tended to feel that she had done rather better than she deserved.

Since it was something she could do on her own, you'd think that Tamie would be thankful that ball-bouncing was popular. Her ball wasn't large and didn't look that wonderful — there was no comical picture of an animal on the side, for example, with a bow tie and yellow waistcoat. But it was firm and hard, and fitted perfectly in her palm. It was faithful, round, and it shone.

ところが、きょう、さっきから、毬はなんとなく弾み方を弱めて来ていた。初めのうちそれは、柔らかすぎる砂地で突く時のような手応えだったから、タミエは場所を変えてみたり、力を入れて突いたりしてごまかしていたのだが、毬はだんだん変な音を立て始め、妙に軟らかな手触りになり出した。もしタミエが真相を見究めることの好きなたちであったなら、強く押しながら表面をもう片方の掌で軽く覆ってみることによって、既にかすかながら空気の洩れる状態になっている箇所を発見したことだろう。しかしタミエはそういうたちでは全然ないので、その不吉な軟らかさが絶望的にまでならないうちに、ひとまず突くのを中止してしまった。毬が弾まなくなるなどというあり得べからざる成行きは無視するのが一番賢明だという風にタミエは思う。さっきから毬の手応えがおかしくなって来たなどということは「なかったこと」にしてしまえばいい、そしてすっかりそんな兆しを忘れ尽してから、さて何事もなかったとして突いてみれば、きっと毬は元通りよく弾むだろう。タミエの掌のくぼみに、きっちりと硬く撥ね返って来るだろう。

But on this particular day the ball seemed a little sluggish. At first, it was rather as though she were bouncing it on soft, sandy ground. So she tried moving elsewhere and throwing the ball down harder, to make it seem that nothing was wrong. But the ball was now starting to make a funny noise, and feeling strangely soft. If Tamie had been the type of child who enjoyed getting at the truth, she would probably have squeezed the ball tight in one palm and run the other gently over its surface, thus detecting the source of a slight leak of air. But Tamie wasn't that type at all, so before the ominous softness had developed too far, she stopped playing. The loss of bounce was something that simply shouldn't happen and it was best ignored. She should act as though the ball had never felt strange at all. Once she had forgotten entirely all signs of strangeness, she would throw the ball again, as though nothing had happened. It would then bounce as it always had, flying firmly back into her palm.

そこでタミエは毬をポケットに入れて歩き出した。ポケットはいつも通り丸く膨んだ。邸の高い石垣に沿って、日の差すことの少ない横道へ外れる。石垣に沿って、といっても、石垣と道との間には、かなりの幅の溝がある。雨でないかぎり殆んど水はなくて、底に芹なんか生え、小蟹がたくさん歩いていたりする。その溝の更に下に、太い土管が埋まっているらしい。そしてそれは、この道の行き止まりから見える濁った大きな川へと注いでいるのである。向う岸は畑であった。いつもいっぱいに陽が当っていて、山羊がいたりした。タミエは川の向うへ行ったことがなく、こっち側もここしか知らない。なぜなら川のこちら側は、少なくともタミエの歩く範囲内では皆家の蔭になっていて、その川に接したところの地所に住む者でなくては川岸に出られないもののようであった。第一、所謂川岸という風な、小石のある砂地や草土手などはまるっきりない様子で、この道のはずれにしても、片側は石垣、片側は竹林が水の際までを囲い、唯一の途切れ目である道と溝との幅は、その間際で俄かに崩れたような工合に終っていて、朽ちかけた杭に錆びた有刺鉄線が絡んでいるあたりはもう川泥の、なかば塵芥捨場の、危なくて汚なくて降りては行けない。でもここはタミエの気に入りの場所の一つで、歩き疲れるとよくここで長いことしゃがんでいた。いつも日の差している明るい向う岸を見るのが好きだった。いつも

Tamie put the ball in her pocket and started to walk. The pocket bulged firm and round as normal. She followed the stone boundary wall of the large garden, turning down into a sunless pathway. Between the wall and the pathway ran a wide ditch. Unless it was raining, the ditch was practically free of water; at the bottom, there were clumps of parsley and lots of little crabs moving about. Apparently, buried beneath the ditch was a large clay pipe that flowed into the muddy waters of the big river you could see from the bottom of the path.

The far side of the river was always bathed in sunlight. There were fields and goats. Tamie had never been over there. And even on this side, she had never seen other parts of the river. It was all blocked by houses, at least as far as she'd ever walked. Unless you lived in one of the houses, there was no way down. There were no grassy banks or stretches of pebbly sand to be seen. Even at the end of the path, there was just the wall on one side and a thick bamboo grove on the other, both of which carried on right to the water's edge. The only view of the river was from the gap formed by the path and the ditch, and these fell abruptly away some distance short of the water, into an area of river mud where people dumped rubbish. The area was fenced off with rusty barbed wire on rotting staves; it was dirty and dangerous and you couldn't get down.

The end of the path was one of Tamie's favourite places and when she was tired of walking she would spend a lot of time there, just sitting on her haunches. She liked looking over at the far bank, bright in the sunshine. She liked looking at the clouds reflected in this small snatch of

左から右へゆっくり動く、僅かばかりの川に雲が映るのを見るのが好きだった。とりわけ夕焼が綺麗だった。けれど今日はやはりポケットが気になって落ち着かず、タミエは夕焼には間のある川を離れて引き返した。

毬を突こうかな。努めてさりげなく、タミエは思った。横道を出てからさっきとは逆へ曲がった。少し行くと四つ角に出る。その一角は松に野藤の絡んだ暗い林で、いつかその奥に、とても大きな鶏位もある鳥が思いがけないほど低い枝に止まっているのを、タミエは見た。タミエが話しても誰も本当にしなかったけれど、本当に鳥はいて、タミエの方をじっと見たのだ。でもタミエだって二度とは見たことがない。雉みたいな顔つきの鳥だったが。今はグミの花ざかり。いつだってタミエはこんな風だ。

毬については、もう今度は疑いようがなかった。哀れな音で弱々しく二つ三つ弾んだあと、毬はあらぬ方へ転がってしまい、拾ったタミエはその裂目を見つけないわけに行かなかった。タミエはそれを空へ投げては受け止めながら、せっせと歩いた。

river, as the water moved slowly from left to right. Sunset was especially beautiful.

But today her mind was on her pocket and she couldn't relax. She left the river well before sunset.

May as well have a bounce, said Tamie to herself, trying to be unconcerned. She came out of the path, back onto the road, and turned in the opposite direction to that from which she had come. After a while she reached a crossroads. On one side was a dark wood of pine trees overgrown with wild wisteria. Tamie had once seen a huge bird here, as big as a rooster, perching on a very low bough. Nobody believed her when she told them, but it was true. The bird was really there. It stared right at her. But she'd not seen it again. Its face was like a pheasant's, she remembered. But now, look at all these silverberry flowers! she thought. Tamie was always like this.

As for the ball, there was no longer any room for doubt. With a melancholy sound, it gave a few feeble bounces and then rolled off in an unexpected direction. Tamie picked it up. She couldn't fail to notice the split now. She walked hurriedly on, tossing the ball up into the air and catching it as she went.

二度とは買ってやらないと、きびしく云い渡されていた。でも、毬はなければならない。よく弾む毬が。タミエの毬が。毬はどこにあるか。勿論玩具屋にあるのだ。タミエは、毬を、新しい裂けていない毬を手に入れようと心に決めたが、タミエが無一文であるからには、手に入れるということは買うこととは違うことだった。

玩具屋はタミエの家の近くにもあった。鯛焼屋と兼業で、菓子と玩具のあいのこのような、食べるような遊ぶような極彩色のあれこれ、それからその時々のはやりの玩具、今なら毬と、男の子がはやらせている銀色の拳銃が山のようにある。でもそこでタミエが毬を「手に入れる」ことはできそうにないので、タミエの足は隣街に向いていた。

隣街へは、一度だけ紛れ込んだことがある。やたらに歩くうち偶然に賑やかな店通りへ出てしまって、なんだか慌てて引き返したことがある。でもちょっと見ただけでも店通りは随分立派で、玩具屋だって二軒も三軒も、ことによったら十軒位もありそうであった。

'I'm not buying you another,' she'd been told sharply.

But she had to have a ball, one that bounced well. *Tamie*'s ball. Where were there balls? At toy shops, of course. She resolved to get a new one, one without a split. But as she had no money, *getting* one wouldn't mean *buying* one.

There was one toy shop near her house. It sold fish-shaped pancakes as well, crammed with sweet bean paste. It stocked all sorts of brightly coloured toys and sweets and combinations of the two. Naturally, it catered for the latest crazes, and so now it had piles of balls and silver-coloured pistols, which were all the rage with boys. But there was no chance of *getting* her ball *there,* so she headed for the next town.

She had been to the next town once before by chance. She had been walking at random and had suddenly found herself in a busy street of shops. A little nervous, she had turned back. But she had seen enough to know that it was rather a splendid place. It would have at least two or three toy shops, perhaps as many as ten.

長いことかかって、それでもまだ日のあるうちに、タミエは見覚えのある角まで来ていた。その細い道の向うを、せわしい夕刻の人の往き交いが見えていた。そこに来るまでタミエは、「手に入れる」ことについては何も考えず、ただ一心に道筋の記憶を追ったり、次の角までに犬に出喰わすかどうかという賭をやったりして来たのだが、いよいよもう表通りの賑わしさは近づいた。右へも左へも途切れ目のわからない遠くまで店並は続いていたが、それまでに出会った猫の毛色による占いだと、タミエは右へ行くべきであった。

二、三軒目にすぐ玩具屋があった。きちんと箱に入ったママゴトのセットだの、着換え付きの睫毛の長い眠り人形だの、螺子で跳び歩く兎の縫いぐるみなどのある大きな店で、もちろん毬も、大きいのや小さいのや色つきのや網袋入のやらが沢山あった。タミエはちょっと立ち止まってみたが、又歩き出してしまった。いろんな店があった。十軒位過ぎると又毬が見えた。文具店なのだが、学童相手に野球や卓球の道具も置いていて、はやりの毬も仕入れたと見える。でもタミエはそこも通り過ぎた。店通りはなかなか尽きない。日が傾き、気早な店には灯が入った。やがて街灯が一斉に明るんだ。次の次ので必らず手に入れよう、とタミエは決めた。

She walked for a long time, but it was still light when she came to a turning she recognised. At the bottom of a narrow path she glimpsed the busy to and fro of the evening crowd. On her way, she hadn't thought at all about getting the ball; she had been trying to remember the route, or betting herself whether she'd meet a dog before the next turning. But now the bustle of the main street was there in front of her. A line of shops stretched out to left and right as far as she could see. On the basis of the colours of the cats she had come across so far, she knew she must turn right.

Just a few stores along, she came to a toy shop — a large one with boxed sets of toy kitchenware, dolls with spare outfits and long-lashed eyes that opened and closed, rabbits that jumped about when you wound them up. And, of course, there were lots of balls as well — big ones, small ones, coloured ones, balls in string bags. Tamie stopped and looked, but then eventually she carried on walking.

There were all sorts of different shops. After passing another ten or so, Tamie noticed more balls. The shop was for stationery really, but it also sold baseball and table-tennis equipment for schoolchildren, and it looked like the owner had decided to stock the rubber balls that were the current craze. But Tamie walked on. The street seemed endless. The sun began to go down and some of the shops were already turning on lights. Eventually, the street lamps came on, all at once. I'll definitely get a ball at the next place but one, Tamie decided.

次の次のは手狭な構えの、人気のない店で、毬は道のきわに、値段の順に積まれていた。タミエは弾むことをやめたポケットの毬を出して左手に持ち、右手で真白な新しいのを一つ持って、大きさを比べるようにして立っていた。毬はちょうど同じ位の大きさである。安い方から二番目の仕切りに入っていたのだが、タミエは絵なんかついた大きすぎるのよりも、小粋で手頃なこの毬がほしい。もし店の人が出て来たら、ちょっと小首を傾げてみせて、ほしいけど今お金を持って来なかった、という風に毬を戻せばいいのである。

奥の居間との仕切りの障子はなかなか開かない。タミエの後を行く人たちも滅法忙しそうで振り向きもしない。タミエはふいに右手をポケットに入れ、その上から左手の毬も入れた。

極めてゆっくり、タミエは店の前を過ぎた。けれど少し行って曲がり角を曲がってからは、全速力で走った。あたりは初めての家並だが、うろつき馴れた勘で行き止まりにならない小路がわかるので、もと来た方角へ、つまり斜め右へ、細い道を何度も折れて走った。或る家からは葱の匂いがする。或る家からは魚を焼く匂いがする。或る家からは醤油の煮立つ匂いがする。

The next place but one was a small store with nobody about. Balls were piled up on the roadside, arranged in order of price. Tamie took the damaged ball from her pocket and held it in her left hand. She picked up a brand-new white ball in her right, and stood as though comparing them. They were almost exactly the same size. The white ball was the second-cheapest type, but it was a nice size and looked good. Tamie preferred it to the ones with pictures on — they were all too big. If someone came out of the shop, she could tilt her head pensively, put the ball back and say she would have liked it, but hadn't brought any money with her.

The screen that separated the sales area from the living quarters at the back of the shop remained shut. None of the busy crowd hurrying along the road turned to look at her. Tamie suddenly slipped her right hand into her pocket. Then, into the same pocket she put the ball she'd been holding in her left hand.

Very slowly, Tamie passed along the front of the shop and farther down the street. But after a short while she turned into a side road, and began to run as fast as she could. The packed rows of houses around her were entirely unfamiliar, but countless hours of wandering about had given her a feel for when an alley was more than just a dead end. Weaving through the narrow streets and alleys she managed to keep running diagonally to the right — the direction from which she had come. She caught the smells of evening cooking as she ran. Spring onions at one house, grilled fish at another, vegetables simmering in soy broth.

ふと、晩春の仄闇の向うに、見知った板塀が見えた。タミエはほっとして走りやめた。もうこれであの大きな鳥のいた藪の四辻まで大して遠くはないし、その先はもう知れている。それでもタミエが今歩いている道はまだ初めて通る道なので、タミエは両側の家々を物珍しく眺めて進んだ。見知った板塀へ曲がる一軒手前は、ごく低い竹の格子垣で、ちょっとした野菜畑を含む平らな庭が見えた。道から手の到くところに、三、四十も実をつけた果樹があった。海近の暖い土地柄とはいえ、この辺は別に柑橘類の栽培はしていないので、タミエは木に生っているのが面白くて傍へ寄った。樹の丈の割に、果実は大変大きく思われた。しかしタミエのポケットの毬よりは少し大き目という位であろうか、八百屋で見る夏蜜柑よりは余程小ぶりである。元来そういう種類なのか、本格的に栽培されたものでないせいなのか、そこのところはよくわからない。ともかく実は鈴生りで、冷くて重くていい匂いである。行き当りばったりのものを「手に入れる」という癖はない方なので、タミエは手に受けて顔を寄せてみただけで又歩き出した。そうしたらふいに呼び留められた。

Suddenly, through the late spring twilight, she saw a timber wall that she recognised. She stopped running and breathed a sigh of relief. It wasn't far now to the crossroads and the wood where she had seen the large bird. From there she'd have no problems. The road she was walking along now, though, was new to her and she looked with curiosity at the houses on either side as she passed. Just before the timber wall, where she was going to turn, was a small house with a modest vegetable garden separated from the road by a low fence of latticed bamboo. In the garden, within arm's reach of the road, was a tree with thirty or forty oranges hanging from its boughs. They caught Tamie's attention. Although the area was near the sea and warm all year, nobody grew much citrus fruit there, so it was unusual to see some on a tree.

She stepped towards the tree. Its small size made the oranges look very large, but, in fact, they were not much bigger than the balls in Tamie's pocket, and much smaller than the summer oranges she saw at the greengrocer's. Perhaps that was because they weren't grown for selling, or perhaps they were just a small variety. It was difficult to tell. But the branches were packed with them. They were heavy and cool to the touch. They smelt beautiful. Tamie wasn't really in the habit of taking things she just happened to come across, so she simply cupped an orange in her hand and leant her face towards it. Then, leaving the orange on the tree, she started to walk away. But just at that moment, somebody called out to her.

急ぎ足に庭を横切って来たのは、頭の丸いずんぐりした着流しの男だったが、その目はすぐ、タミエの膨れたポケットに向いていた。欲しければ上げるよ。ちょうど取りに来たところだ。男は手にした花鋏をタミエに突きつけるようにした。タミエはポケットから毬を二つ出して見せようかとちょっと思案したが、その毬のいかがわしいことにかけては、果実を取り出してみせることより大してましとも思えなかった。

男は一つ切ってタミエにくれ、又上げるからね、黙って取るんじゃないぞ、と云った。たくさん貰ってどうもありがとう、とタミエは云ったものである。曲がって、男の家が見えなくなってから、タミエは皮に爪を立てた。夕闇の道で、果実は高く香った。歩きながら食べた。熱心に食べた。

私は本当は、タミエがその強い酸味と芳香とに感動してしまって、もう一度取って返し、男の立ち去ったあとの果樹の根本に、真白な毬を——タミエにとってほんとうに欲しかった大切なものの方を——こっそり置いて去るという風に書きたかったのだが、タミエはそんなことをしなかったのだから仕方がない。

A small, stocky, round-faced man was hurrying across the garden in her direction. His eyes went straight to her bulging pocket.

'If you want some, all you have to do is ask,' he said, jabbing the sharp end of his pruners towards her. 'I've just come out to pick them.'

For a moment, Tamie considered whether she might bring the two balls out of her pocket to show him. But given what she had done, producing the balls from her pocket didn't seem much better than producing oranges.

The man cut an orange from the tree and gave it to her.

'I'll give you another next time. Don't just help yourself!'

'You're so generous!' said Tamie. 'Thank you!'

She turned the corner and, once she was out of sight of the man's house, she pressed her nails into the rind of the fruit. Its fragrance rose powerfully into the evening air over the pathway. She ate the orange as she walked along. She ate greedily.

What I wanted to write was that Tamie, moved by the intense, sharp taste and beautiful smell of the orange, went straight back, after the man had left, and quietly placed the bright white ball — the precious object that she had wanted so much — at the foot of the orange tree. But she didn't, and so I can't.

　タミエがあの暮れおちた川の覗き口に捨てたのは、裂け掛けた古い毬と、思いがけない取得物であった柑橘類の食べ殻の方であって、タミエのポケットには、そこらの泥で巧みによごしたよく弾む毬がちゃんと入っていたのである。そして誰一人その秘かないきさつに気づいた者はなかったのであるが、又しても例のうろんさは、その宵のタミエに沁みていた芳香性の柑橘類の残り香と共に、不確かに甘酸っぱく匂って止まなかった。

What she did was return in the darkness to her river-viewing point, and there dispose of the split ball and the peel of the unexpectedly acquired orange. The new ball was safely in her pocket, now skilfully smeared with mud.

Nobody knew anything of these secret goings-on, but together with the scent of citrus that clung to Tamie that night, there lingered, as always, the vague, bitter-sweet smell of suspicion.

江國香織　Kaori Ekuni

1964年東京生まれ。2004年直木賞をはじめ、数多くの文学賞を受賞している。英語で読むことのできる作品に『Twinkle Twinkle（きらきらひかる）』、『God's Boat（神様のボート）』等がある。「サマーブランケット」は、2002年山本周五郎賞を受賞した『泳ぐのに、安全でも適切でもありません』に収録されている。「サマーブランケット」の英訳は、第5回しずおか世界翻訳コンクールの最優秀賞受賞作に基づく。

Kaori Ekuni was born in Tokyo in 1964. Awards include the 2004 Naoki Prize. Works published in English include the novels *Twinkle Twinkle* and *God's Boat*. 'Summer Blanket' is from her Shugoro Yamamoto Prize-winning 2002 collection *Oyogu no ni anzen demo tekisetsu demo arimasen* (*Not Safe or Suitable for Swimming*). The English version is based on a Grand Prize-winning entry to the 2004/5 Shizuoka International Translation Competiton.

サマーブランケット

Summer Blanket

江國香織

Kaori Ekuni

海のそばの家には、砂がたくさん入ってくる。マリウスが砂浜を走りまわってくるせいもあるが、それよりも、しじゅう窓をあけているせいだろう。ことにいまの季節は。

昼間は、太陽の匂いがする。砂と、温められた木と、干からびたペンキの匂いもする。夜になると、潮の匂いが俄然生気を帯びる。水と冷えた空気と、海辺の生き物たちのつくりだす匂い。それは、ある種の果実が、熟れすぎて腐る直前に放つ匂いと似ている。

家の中で、私はいちにちじゅう、それらの匂いをかぐ。

海のそばの家に、こうまでたくさんの砂が入ってくることを、私がここを買う前に、誰か教えてくれればよかったのにと思う。思うけれど、思っても仕方のないことだ。私がこの家に暮らして、じき三年になる。

私には家族はいない。父も母も死んでしまったし、独身で、ゴールデン・レトリーバーのマリウスと、二人きりで暮らしている。マリウスは老犬で、獣医に言わせると「動脈硬化を起こしかけている」。

Houses by the sea get full of sand. This is certainly true of mine. Much of it is brought in by Marius when he comes back from running around on the beach. But I think even more is blown in through the windows, especially at this time of year. I always leave them open.

In the daytime the sun permeates everything. There is the smell of the sand, of wood in the heat, of dried paint. At nightfall, suddenly the smells of the sea prevail: the smell of water, of cool air, of the creatures of the shore. They are strong and pervasive, like the odour of an overripe fruit just before it starts to rot.

I live surrounded by these smells.

I wish someone had told me about the sand before I bought the place. But wishing won't change anything. I have lived here almost three years now.

I have no family: I am not married, and my mother and father are both dead. I live with Marius, my golden retriever — just the two of us. Marius is old and the vet says his arteries are beginning to harden.

私には友達が二人いる。その二人とは、去年の夏に出会った。出会ったというより、彼らが、ある日突然この海辺の家に——そして私の人生に——、やってきたのだった。

まゆきちゃんはすとんとした体型の、いまふうの女の子だ。ショートパンツから伸びる長い脚に、私はしばしば見とれてしまう。大森くんは彼女のボーイフレンドで、南の島の住人かと思うほど日に灼けている。二人とも、この家からバスで二十分ほどの場所にある大学の学生だ。

彼らは毎週水曜日に連れだってやってくる。そのほかの日も、気が向けばふらりと遊びに来る。いつでもいらっしゃい。私は彼らにそう言っている。

きょうは波が高い。私は昼食のあとずっと、マイケル・ギルモアの小説を読んでいた。厚くて重い、でも興味深い小説だ。私が寝そべって本を読んでいるソファの足元で、マリウスは眠っている。古めかしい木製の側卓は、ゴミ置き場から拾ってきたものだ。あんまりいいものが捨ててあったので、びっくりして拾った。

I have two friends, whom I met last year. Well I say 'met', but actually they just turned up one day at my house; they have been part of my life ever since.

Mayuki, like a lot of Japanese girls these days, is quite tall and very slender. When she wears shorts I often find myself gazing at her long legs. Omori is her boyfriend. He is so tanned one would think him an inhabitant of a tropical island. They are both students at a local university, about twenty minutes from here by bus.

They come to my house every Wednesday — and on other days as well, if they feel like it. Come any time, I tell them.

The sea was rough. Since lunchtime I had been lying on the sofa, reading a novel by Mikal Gilmore — a big, heavy book, but very interesting. Marius was sleeping beside the sofa on the floor, next to an old-fashioned wooden side table that someone had put out with the rubbish. Astonished to find something of such good quality thrown away, I picked it up and brought it home.

私は腕時計を見た。二時半。もうすぐ大森くんが来ることになっている。

頁をめくろうとして、本まで砂でざらついていることに気づいた。私は自分の怠惰に笑ってしまう。実際、ここに越してから私は滅多に掃除をしない。窓枠や床ばかりか、バスタブの中もシーツもざらついている。それで私は欧米人のように、家の中でも靴をはいて暮らすようになった。慣れてしまえば、むしろその方が性に合っていた。靴を脱ぐ、というのはひどく無防備になる行為だ。

「掃除、しましょうか？」

まゆきちゃんはときどきそう言ってくれる。そのたびに私は、大げさに手と頭を両方ふって断る。いいのいいの、そのうちするから、と。

まゆきちゃんはのんびりした、やさしい子だ。東京の子で、いまは大学のそばの「コーポ」というところに、一人で住んでいるという。大森くんは地元の子で、ここからそう遠くない場所にある家に、両親と住んでいる。

I looked at my watch. Two-thirty. Omori would be here soon.

Turning the page, I noticed that the book was rough with sand. I smiled at my indolence. I have hardly cleaned the place at all since I came here. The window frames, the floor — even the bath and sheets — everything feels gritty. With all this sand about, I have taken to wearing my shoes indoors, like a Westerner. In fact, now that I am used to it, I feel it suits my character. Taking off one's shoes leaves one terribly defenceless.

'Shall I do some cleaning?' Mayuki sometimes asks.

Oh no! I say, waving my hands and shaking my head exaggeratedly. Don't worry about that. I'll get round to it.

Mayuki is a kind, easy-going girl from Tokyo. Now she is living in some kind of accommodation next to the university. A 'co-po', she calls it. Omori is a local boy; he lives with his parents in a house not far from here.

一度、まゆきちゃんが高校時代の友達を数人連れて、大森くん抜きで遊びに来たことがある。花火をたくさん持ってきていて、道子さんも一緒にしましょう、と言った。私たちは海辺でそれをした。友達の中の一人を、まゆきちゃんは「元彼」だと言った。その「元彼」は大柄で色の白い、育ちのよさそうな子だったけれど、なんとなくふにゃっとした印象だった。私は心の中でまゆきちゃんに、大森くんのがいいわね、と、言った。まゆきちゃんは彼らに、

「道子さんはお嬢さんなの」

と説明した。

「いまどきいないような、本物のお嬢さんなの」

と。

たしかに、私の両親は裕福だった。それで私は、家政婦も運転手もいる家庭で育った。大学を卒業して就職したが、両親が死ぬと遺産が残り、私は二十年勤めた会社を辞めて、海辺に家を買って引越した。でも、と、あのとき私は不思議な気持ちがしたものだ。でも、「お嬢さん」でいるというのがどういうものか、まゆきちゃんにはきっと決してわかってもらえないだろう。

Mayuki once came without Omori, bringing a group of old high-school friends. They had fireworks on the beach and Mayuki asked me to join them. She described one of the group as her 'ex'. He was a large, pale-skinned boy. He looked well-brought-up, but there was something rather insipid about him. You're better off with Omori, I said silently to Mayuki.

'Michiko's a lady,' she explained to her friends. 'A real old-fashioned lady.'

It is true that my parents were well off. When I was a child we had a housekeeper and a driver. After university I got a job,and stayed with it for twenty years. When my parents died, though, and I inherited their money, I left the job and bought this house by the sea. *But,* I thought... It felt odd to be spoken of like that. I am sure Mayuki could never understand what it is like to be a woman brought up in that way.

そして、そういうとき、私はまゆきちゃんに対し、恨みがましい気持ちを抱いてしまうのに気づく。いわれのない、でも見まがいようのない、恨みがましさ。私は恥入り、動揺する。

むし暑い午後だ。私は本を閉じ、台所——狭いが風が通るので、居間よりはすこし涼しい——にいって、アイスティをつくる。

二十六歳から三十九歳までの年月、私は、上司であり父の友人でもあった男性と不倫関係にあった。彼は素晴らしい男性で、私は彼を、心から愛した。そのことは、でも、もう思い出さないようにしている。彼は妻の元に戻った。つまりそういうことだ。

私は、彼の写真を一枚、この家に飾っている。未練というのではなく、なんというか、私の人生の彩りのために。

ここでの生活は、単調だけれど満足のいくものだ。私には、これから一生かかっても読みきれないだろうほどの、かつて読んだ本がある。レコードも二百枚ほど持っている。

At times like this, I notice myself feeling resentful of Mayuki — unjustifiably, yet quite unmistakeably resentful. It shames and upsets me.

It was a hot and humid afternoon. I closed my book and went to the kitchen. It is a small room, but it gets a breeze, so it's a little cooler than the living room. I made some iced tea.

From the age of twenty-six until I was thirty-nine, I had an affair with my boss — a friend of my father's. He was a wonderful man, and I loved him deeply. But I try not to think about it. He went back to his wife. That is all there is to it.

I keep a photograph of him on display in the house. I put it there not because I haven't got over him, but rather, as it were, to give some colour to my existence.

Life here is monotonous, but satisfying. I have a lot of books I've read in the past — I'll never be able to read them all again, even if I keep at it for the rest of my life. I also have about two hundred records.

私が四十二歳のときに父が死に、その翌年に母が死んだ。あれこれ処分すると、遺産はかなりな金額になった。私の名義になっている不動産などもあり、それも一緒に売ってもらった。それらの整理や父の会社の様々な手続き——私はいまも役員の一人になっている。名前だけのことだ——がすむと、私は軽い鬱病になった。薬がなければ眠れなくなり、死ぬことばかり考えた。思いつめるというのではなく、ふいに、ぱっくりとその考えが口をあけ、そこにぐらりと傾くのだ。

恋人を失ったときには罹らなかった鬱病などという病気に、両親を失ったときに罹ったという事実は、私をまったく打ちのめした。

オプタリドン、ハイミナール、そして、青い小さなハルシオンの粒たち。私にとって薬はもっとも親しいものになった。

ただし副作用も強く、私はしばしば昏倒した。でも構わなかった。痛くはなかったし、あちこちに痣をつくったが、私の身体に関心を持つ人など、この世に一人もいないことがわかっていた。

いまでもときどき指の先が白くなり、痺れて動かなくなる。チック症状がでることもある。でも、ここに引越して一年もすると、私は薬をのまなくなっていた。

My father died when I was forty-two; my mother, a year later. Their estates amounted to a considerable inheritance. I had everything sold, including some property that was in my own name. There were also a number of steps to be taken in relation to my father's company (I am still a director, though only in name). Once all that was done, I developed a mild depression. I could not sleep without drugs, and I kept thinking about dying. I didn't brood on it; it would just suddenly appear in my mind, like a gaping hole. I felt myself lurching towards it.

It was a terrible shock to me that I should suffer from depression when I lost my parents. I had not suffered from it at all when I lost my lover.

Optalidon, Quaalude and small blue tablets called Halcion — these drugs became my closest friends.

They had strong side effects, though, and I often fainted. But that didn't matter. Falling didn't hurt, and although I got some bruises, I knew there was nobody in the world who cared what state my body was in.

Even now, I sometimes lose feeling in the tips of my fingers — they turn white and I cannot move them. I also get a nervous twitch occasionally. But I had stopped taking the drugs within a year of moving here.

マリウスが死んだら、と考えることがある。マリウスが死んだら、私を地上につなぎとめるものは何もなくなる。

大森くんは、三時すぎに自転車でやってきた。Tシャツに短パンという恰好で、腕や額に汗をかいて。

「こんちはー」

あかるい声で言い、玄関ではなく庭から入ってきた。

「ごくろうさま。わざわざごめんなさい」

私は言い、ドッグフードを受け取った。それから台所に戻り、大森くんにアイスティをだす。

私の家には、あまりいろいろな種類の飲み物がない。それで大森くんにもまゆきちゃんにも、いつも紅茶をだす。さいわい、二人とも私の紅茶を気に入ってくれている。ことにまゆきちゃんは気に入ってくれていて、どうやって作るのかと尋ねられた。ブランデーシュガーを使っていると説明すると、彼らは二人とも、ブランデーシュガーを知らないと言った。私はそのとき、自分が過去の遺物であるような気がした。

「暑いー。夏みたいだな」

大森くんは言い、Tシャツの裾をめくりあげて顔をぬぐった。やせていて臍のまるい、日に灼けた腹があらわになった。

「夏よ、もう」

I sometimes think about Marius dying. When he dies, there'll be nothing left to bind me to the world.

Omori arrived by bicycle just after three o'clock. He wore a T-shirt and shorts. There was sweat on his forehead and arms.

'Hi!' he said brightly, coming in via the garden, rather than the front door.

'Thank you,' I said, taking the dog food he had brought. 'I'm sorry to put you to so much trouble.' I went back into the kitchen and got him some iced tea.

I don't have many drinks in the house and I always give Omori and Mayuki my special-recipe Indian tea. Luckily, they both like it — especially Mayuki, who once asked me how I made it. Neither of them had heard of the type of sugar I used. It made me feel like a relic of a past age.

'Whew! It's so hot!' said Omori. 'Like summer!'

Lifting the front of his T-shirt to wipe his face, he revealed his round navel, his slim, tanned stomach.

'It *is* summer,' I said.

二人がこの家にやってくるようになってから、もうじき一年になるのだ。

毎週一度、水曜日に買物に行くことにしていた。海岸ぞいに二十分歩くとバス停があり、そこからバスに十五分乗れば、町につく。比較的大きな町で、必要なものはたいてい手に入る。

その日、家をでるとポーチにまゆきちゃんが足をなげだしてすわっていた。そばに大森くんがいて、海に遊びに来て貧血をおこしたのだと説明した。私の家の玄関が、いちばん近い日陰だったのだ、と。まゆきちゃんは、どういうわけか膝にタオルハンカチをひろげていて、大丈夫、と言った。もうなおるから大丈夫、と。私は二人を居間に通した。まゆきちゃんをソファにすわらせて休ませ、氷水をコップに入れて手渡した。

その日、大森くんはまゆきちゃんを送っていくついでに、私を町まで車に乗せてくれた。このあたりの海は子供の時分から遊び場だったし、まゆきちゃんともよく来るのだと言った。私がいつも海岸ぞいに二十分歩いてバス停にいき、バスで買物に行くと話すと同情してくれた。しょっちゅう来るから、週に一度くらいなら送りますよ、と言い、私は、人の好意に甘えるのは好きじゃないの、とこたえた。大森くんは眉を持ち上げて不思議そうな顔をつくったあとで微笑んで、それ以上何も言わなかった。

Almost a year has passed since the two of them came here for the first time.

It was a Wednesday, my regular shopping day. Ordinarily, I would walk along the coast for twenty minutes and then take a fifteen-minute bus ride to the town. It is a reasonably large place and one can get most things one requires.

That day, I came out of the house to find Mayuki sitting in the porch, her legs stretched out in front of her. Omori was beside her. He explained that she had begun to feel faint on the beach, and that my porch had been the nearest shade they could find.

'I'm okay,' said Mayuki, for some reason holding a pocket towel over her knees. 'I'm feeling better already.'

I took them into the living room. I got Mayuki to relax on the sofa and gave her a glass of iced water.

When Omori took her home, he gave me a lift to the town. He told me that he had been coming to the beach here since he was a child, and now he often came with Mayuki. He sympathised with me when I told him how I walked twenty minutes to the bus stop to go shopping.

'If it's just once a week, I'll take you,' he said. 'I come here so often, anyway.'

'I don't like to take advantage of people's kindness,' I said.

He gave a puzzled look, eyebrows raised. Then he smiled, but didn't say anything more.

ところが翌週の水曜日、まるで約束をしていたみたいにあたりまえの顔で、こんちは、と言って二人連れだってやってきた。結局、そういうことになった。壜入りのバルサミコ酢やドッグフードを、荷物の重さを考えずに買えるのは実際ありがたいことだった。

彼らは若くて、きれいなカップルだ。とても仲がいい。部屋から部屋へ移動するのに、ごく自然に手をつなぐ。それは微笑ましい光景だ。

彼らはそうやって連れだって、興味深そうに私の部屋を眺める。私の部屋を、そして人生を。

「御主人ですか？」

私を捨てて家庭に帰ってしまった男の写真をみて、あるときまゆきちゃんが尋ねた。

「ええ」

私は、愛に満ちた家庭を築いてきた女みたいにこたえた。

「先に死んでしまったの。歳が随分離れてたから」

その嘘は、何の罪悪感もひき起こさなかった。言った途端に、ほんとうのことのように思えた。

The next Wednesday, there they both were. 'Hi!' they said nonchalantly, as though they were expected. And they kept on coming every week. It turned out to be a blessing: it meant I could buy dog food and bottles of balsamic vinegar without worrying about the weight.

They are an attractive young couple, very happy together. They hold hands spontaneously, as they move from room to room. It is lovely to watch.

As they walk around, they take a great interest in my rooms — and my life.

'Is that your husband?' Mayuki once asked, looking at the photograph of the man who had left me to return to his family.

'Yes,' I said, in the manner of a woman who had built a home full of love. 'He died. He was much older than me.'

I didn't feel guilty telling this lie. It seemed like the truth once I'd said it.

まゆきちゃんは犬が好きだ。
「マリウスと遊んでもいいですか？」
そう言って、大森くんと砂浜にでていくこともあった。海で泳いだあと、彼らは濡れたままの身体でやってきて、
「シャワー借りてもいいですか」
と、訊いたりもする。それはたしかに、私の考えでは厚かましいふるまいなのだが、その厚かましさはなにか輝かしい、胸のすくような厚かましさだった。
泳いだあと、彼らの頬は上気していて、まるでセックスのあとのようにみちたりてみえる。
彼ら二人は、私がいままでの人生で、一度も出会ったことのない種類の若者に思える。あるいはいっそ——奇妙なことだが——私は、いままでの人生で出会った若者をすべて忘れてしまったと思える。
水曜日の買物について、せめてアルバイトということにして欲しい、と私が提案すると、二人はその場で相談し、じゃあそうさせてもらいます、と、こたえた。

Mayuki likes dogs.

'Can we play with Marius?' she says, and they take him off to the beach.

Sometimes, they turn up dripping wet from a swim in the sea.

'Can we use the shower?' they ask.

To my way of thinking, this is certainly presumptuous; but it is a rather splendid, refreshing type of presumption.

After they have been swimming their cheeks glow. They look satisfied, as if they have just made love.

They seem to be young people of a type I have never come across before. Or perhaps the strange truth is I have forgotten all the other young people I have ever met.

I asked if I could at least pay them for their help with my shopping on Wednesdays. They conferred for a moment and then replied. Well, if that's okay with you, they said.

「ごちそうさまでした」

アイスティのグラスをテーブルに戻して、大森くんが言った。

「ちゃりで来たからすごく喉かわいてた」

うすいTシャツが汗で背中にはりついている。背骨のかたちが見えるような気がした。

「オレンジ、よかったら持って帰って」

砂ぼこりだらけのテーブルに、オレンジが三つ、ころがっていた。

「これ、何ですか？」

たたんだまま床にどさりと置いてある紺色の物体をみて、大森くんが訊いた。

「ああそれ、サマーブランケット」

私はこたえ、首をすくめた。そんなものを買ってしまったことを恥じている、そういうつもりの仕草だった。

「ここに引越すとき、新しいものは何も買わなかったのに、それだけ衝動買いしてしまったの。なんだか、海辺の家に似合う気がして」

言い訳のようにそう説明した。

それは、紺色の太い木綿糸で編まれた、ずっしりと持ち重りのするブランケットだった。キングサイズなので、困るほど大きい。

「でも使いみちがないの」

私は言い、ばかみたいねとつけたした。

'Thanks,' said Omori, putting his empty iced tea glass back on the table. 'Coming by bike made me really thirsty.'

He was still sweaty, his thin T-shirt clinging to his back. I thought I could make out his spine.

'Take the oranges home with you, if you like,' I said.

There were three oranges lying on the sandy table top.

'What's this?' he asked, looking at some dark blue material, folded up and dumped on the floor.

'Oh, that... It's called a summer blanket,' I said, shrugging. I wanted to show that I was embarrassed to have bought such a thing.

'It was an impulse buy,' I explained as though in justification, 'the only thing I bought when I moved. I thought it would suit a seaside home.'

It was a heavy blanket made of thick blue cotton thread. King-size — hopelessly large.

'But I can't see anything to do with it,' I said.

Stupid, isn't it? I added.

「何のためのものかしら。全然実用的じゃないの」

編み目があらく、それ自体が非常に重いので、ベッドやソファの覆いにすると、だらんとのびてしまってだらしがない。身体にかけるには大きすぎるし、重すぎる。編み目のすきまが大きいので、空気も砂も通してしまう。一人でたたむのさえままならないのだ。

大森くんは私の話を最後まできくと、やせた頬をくぼませて笑った。

「使いましょうか」

たのしそうな口調で言う。

「これ全然使えますよ」

大森くんはその大きな濃紺のかたまりを両腕で抱え、先に立って玄関から外にでた。

海は凪いでいた。

まったく信じ難いことだが、私は家から十分ほどの場所で、大森くんと一緒にサマーブランケットにくるまっている。まったく信じ難いことだが、灰色の砂はかわいていてあたたかく、ブランケットも、木綿とは思えないほどあたたかい。それに大森くんの体温ときたら——。

I carried on: 'I can't imagine what it's for. It's not at all practical. It looks terrible as a throw on a bed or a sofa — the stitching is coarse and so heavy that it stretches.... It's too big and heavy to lie under, and the gaps between the stitches are so wide they let air and sand through. I can't even fold it properly on my own.'

Omori listened to all this and then smiled, deep cracks forming in his thin cheeks.

'Shall we use it now?' he said cheerfully. 'I'm sure we can!'

He picked up the navy blue heap in both arms and led the way out through the hallway.

The sea was calm.

It was totally unbelievable, but there I was, ten minutes from my house, wrapped up in the summer blanket with Omori. It was totally unbelievable, but the grey sand was dry and warm, and the blanket so warm you wouldn't think it was cotton, and then there was the heat of Omori's body....

そろそろ夕方だというのに、太陽はまだ白くあかるい。

「こうやって、おもてで使えばいいんですよ、きっと」

大森くんは実に無造作に、砂に直接それをひろげた。

「でけえ」

感心したようにつぶやいて横になり、私にも横になるよう促した。私はすでに動揺していた。こんなことは困る、と思ったし、表情も動作も、戸惑うというよりこわばっていただろう。大森くんのゴム草履が、砂にすこし埋もれてころがっている。

「道子さんも早く」

さらに促され、私はしぶしぶ靴を脱いだ。

横になると、大森くんは私の上にかぶさるようにしてブランケットの端を持ち、二つ折りにして、二人でくるまれるようにした。

「これ、でかいからいいですよ。こんなふうにできるもん。衝動買いして正解です」

私はじっとしていた。息さえもつめていた。うつぶせの姿勢で、海ではなく砂をみていた。砂と紺色の毛布を。

右腕が、大森くんの左腕に触れていた。

It was getting towards evening, but the sun was still white and bright.

'It'll be best to use it like this, outside,' said Omori. He spread the blanket out casually on the sand, then looked at it admiringly.

'It's huge!' he said, as though to himself. Then he lay down.

He urged me to lie down too. I was upset. I can't do this, I thought. I could feel my face and limbs stiffen. Omori's flip-flops lay untidily beside him, partially covered in sand.

'Come on, Michiko!' he urged again. 'Quickly!'

I reluctantly removed my shoes and lay down. Omori leant across me, took the far edges of the blanket and folded it back over us, so that it was wrapped right around us.

'If it wasn't so big, we wouldn't be able to do this,' he said. 'You were right to buy it — a great impulse.'

I kept still, hardly breathing. I was lying on my front. I wasn't looking at the sea, but at the sand. The sand and the blue blanket. My right arm was touching Omori's left.

「砂の匂い」

私が言うと、大森くんは理解できない顔をした。でも、私にはこのとき、砂にも匂いのあることがはっきりとわかった。

「まぶしいのね」

マリウスが水際を歩いているのがみえた。私は目をとじ、なぜだか居間の写真の男のことを思った。私の知っている唯一の男のことを。腕の太い男だった。頭のいい、しずかな話し方をする——。私を抱いているとき、しばしば心からの口調で、いま死ねたらなあ、と言ってくれた。

あのころ、両親は私に散々見合いをさせたが、骨折り損だった。私には、彼以外の男など考えられなかった。それはいまでも変っていない。というより、時間がたつにつれ、その思いは強くなっている。

みずみずしく鮮烈な香りがして、横をみると大森くんがオレンジをむいていた。皮から霧のように果汁がとぶ。爪も指も、したたる汁にだらだらと濡れ、私は大森くんの手に見とれた。なんてきれいな指だろう。

ふいに、速い動作で大森くんが両手をのばした。ブランケットが濡れないように、砂の上でむいているのだった。

'The smell of sand,' I said.

Omori's face was blank, uncomprehending. But at that moment I knew for sure that sand has its own smell.

'The sun's so bright, isn't it?' I said.

I could see Marius walking along the water's edge. I closed my eyes and, for some reason, thought of the man whose photograph was in my living room. He was the only man I had known. He had thick, strong arms; he was clever and softly spoken. When we made love, he would say he wished he could die just then, as we embraced. He said it as though he meant it.

My parents made me go through an endless series of meetings with prospective husbands. It was a waste of effort. I could think of no man but him. I still can't. In fact, as time has passed, this feeling has strengthened.

I noticed a fresh, juicy smell and turned my eyes. Omori was peeling an orange. A mist-like spray radiated from its skin. I gazed at his hands. His fingers and nails were dripping with juice...his beautiful fingers.

Suddenly, he thrust his hands away. He wanted to peel the orange over the sand, so that the juice would not get onto the blanket.

「かまわないから毛布の上でむいて。敷物だもの」

私は言った。

「そのためのものでしょう？」

大森くんは私をみる。傾き始めた日ざしに、まぶしそうに目をほそめた。

オレンジはぬるく、甘かった。私たちは両手をべたべたにしてそれを食べた。

「うらやましいですよ」

大森くんがぼそっと言った。

「道子さんまだ若いのに、悠々自適で、自由で」

自由。

私は微笑み、何も言わなかった。

「まゆきもすげえうらやましがってる。あたしもあんなお嬢さんに生まれたかった、って」

海辺の家は、私そのものみたいだ。窓も戸もあけっぱなしで、砂だらけで、ただじっと建っている。壊れるときまで、何年も何年も。

'Don't worry. Peel it here. It's just a rug,' I said. 'That's what it's for, isn't it?'

He looked at me, his eyes narrow against the light. The sun was now beginning to set.

The orange was warm and sweet. It made our hands sticky as we ate it.

'I'm jealous of you,' said Omori quietly. 'You're still young, but you can do just as you like. You're free.'

Free.

I smiled and said nothing.

'Mayuki's dead jealous as well. She says she wishes she'd been born a lady, like you.'

It is as though the seaside house and I are one and the same. Here we are, covered in sand, windows and doors all open. And here we will stay for years and years, until we collapse.

ふいに耐えがたい思いにかられ、私は立ちあがり、服をはたいた。いそいで靴をはく。

「もう行きましょう」

あたりにはオレンジの香りが残っていて、私たちは二人とも、そのおなじ汁で手や顔をべたべたにしている。

大森くんの体温に、もう一度触れたい強い欲望にかられた。風が髪をばさばさささせて吹きすぎていく。私は腕時計をみないように気をつけた。空はもう青くないが、まだ十分にあかるい。ここにきて、たいして時間はたっていないだろう。その短さを、知りたくはなかった。

毛布はあいかわらず重く、編み目がのびてたるむので扱いづらかった。私たちは両側からそれを持ち、おおざっぱにたたんだ。

「マリウース！」

大森くんが呼び、私たちは砂浜を歩いた。砂だらけの、海辺の家にむかって。

Suddenly, I was overcome. I couldn't bear it. I stood up and wiped the sand from my clothes. I hurriedly put on my shoes.

'Let's go,' I said.

The smell of orange lingered. Our hands and faces were sticky from its juice — the same juice.

I suddenly yearned to feel the warmth of Omori's body once again. The wind blew, tousling my hair. I avoided looking at my watch. The sky was no longer blue, but it was still light. We could only have been there a short time. I didn't want to know how short.

It was a struggle to deal with the heavy blanket. Its stitching stretched and sagged. We each took one side and folded it up roughly.

'Marius!' Omori shouted.

We walked along the sandy beach. Towards the sand-filled seaside house.

角田光代　Mitsuyo Kakuta

1967年神奈川県生まれ。2005年直木賞をはじめ数多くの文学賞を受賞している。テレビドラマや映画化された作品も多い。英語で読むことのできる作品に『Woman on the Other Shore（対岸の彼女）』、『The Eighth Day（八日目の蝉）』等がある。「かなたの子」は2012年泉鏡花文学賞を受賞した同名の作品の表題作。

Mitsuyo Kakuta was born in Kanagawa Prefecture in 1967. Awards include the 2005 Naoki Prize. A number of her works have been adapted for television and cinema. Works available in English include *The Eighth Day* and *Woman on the Other Shore*. 'Kanata no Ko'（'The Child Over There'）is from a collection of the same name that won the Izumi Kyoka Prize in 2012.

かなたの子

The Child Over There

角田光代

Mitsuyo Kakuta

生まれるより先に死んでしまった子に名前などつけてはぜったいにいけない、というのが、その付近での了解ごとだった。あんたはよそものだから知らないだろうけれどまちがっても名前なんかつけるんじゃないよ、呼んだりするんじゃないよと、真一の母親も言っていた。だけどなんといって話しかけたらいいのだろうかと文江は思う。話しかけたりなんかせず、次の子を待てときっと真一もその母も言うだろうが、それじゃあまるでなんにもいなかったみたいだ。

このあたりの人たちは、生まれなかった子は次に生まれてくると信じている。けれど文江はそう思わない。死んだ子と、次に生まれてくる子は別の子なのに違いない。また、八月も腹のなかにいた子が、そもそもいなかったとは文江には思えない。だからこっそり、如月、と名づけた。男か女か教えてもらえなかったが、その月に生まれるはずだったから。死んで腹から出てきた子どもは、真一の先祖が眠る墓に埋められた。菓子も、玩具も、そなえてはいけないと真一の母は言う。彼方の世界にいけないからだそうだ。彼方の世界にいけないと、次に生まれてくることもできないらしい。

One must never give a name to a child that dies before it is born. Everyone in the village understood that. You're not from 'round here so you wouldn't know, said Shinichi's mother, but don't give it a name and don't call out to it. But then how can I talk to it? thought Fumie. Shinichi and his mother would tell her not to talk to it, tell her to wait for the next time around. But if she didn't talk to the child, it would be like it had never existed.

People around there believed that babies that hadn't been born this time would be born the next. But Fumie didn't. She was sure that any child she might have next time would be different to the dead child. And she couldn't think that the child that had been inside her for eight months had never existed. So secretly, she gave it a name. She hadn't been told whether it was a boy or a girl, so she named it Kisaragi, after the second month of the lunar calendar, because that's when it would have been born. The child that had come dead from her belly was buried in the grave of Shinichi's ancestors. Shinichi's mother said she mustn't put sweets or toys by the grave. That would only stop the child getting to the world over there, and if it didn't get to the world over there, it wouldn't be able to be born next time around.

ではうまれるはずの子が生まれず、次の子も生まれなかった場合、その子はどうなるのか、文江はだれにも訊いたことがない。ほかの親のもとに生まれるのだろうか。

子を食べる鬼の話も、嫁いではじめて聞いた。このあたりでは、生まれてすぐ死んでしまった子は、鬼に魅入られ食べられたと言われる。鬼に食べられるなんておそろしいと、身ごもったばかりの文江が言うと、真一も義母も、うちはだいじょうぶだと笑った。彼らが言うには、鬼だって情けがないわけではない、はじめての子はまず食わない。あの家は五人、六人と子がいる、だったらひとりくらい食ったってかまわないと、鬼のほうだってきちんと算段して食らうのだと言うのである。しかし饅頭や握り飯じゃあるまいし、充分だからもう不要なんてことはなかろうに、五人目だろうが六人目だろうが親はかなしかろうに、と文江は思ったが、口には出さなかった。口にしたって、真一や義母が子を食らう鬼を退治できるはずもない。

Fumie had never asked what happened to the child if there wasn't a next time. Would it be born to other parents?

The demon that ate babies — that was something else she'd never heard of before she came to the village as a bride. People in the area said that children that died soon after birth had been bewitched and eaten by a demon. Fumie was horrified. She was already with child when she heard. But Shinichi and his mother laughed. We'll be all right, they said. The demon won't eat a firstborn. He's not that unfeeling. He works it out. They've got five or six in that family already, he says to himself, so it'll do no harm if I have one of theirs. But children aren't rice balls or *manju,* thought Fumie. It's not a question of having enough and not needing any more. Whether it's the fifth or the sixth, or whatever, the parents would still be sad. But she didn't say anything. There was no point. Shinichi and his mother wouldn't be able to destroy a demon that fed on babies.

朝、真一と義母とともに田畑に出て作業をし、昼どき、食事を作りに帰る道すがら、文江はこっそり墓に寄る。寺の裏の、山の斜面にまばらに墓石が立っている。如月の名が刻まれた墓石はもちろんないけれどしゃがんで手を合わせ、如月、如月、と呼びかける。呼びかけるだけで、次に言葉が続かない。道すがらにもいだみかんを供えることもあれば、れんげの花を手向けることもある。如月、お食べ、だの、如月、きれいだね、だの、そういうときだけ、向ける言葉が浮かぶ。そうしていると気持ちが落ち着く。生まれなかった子が、煙の向こうからゆっくり近づいてくるように、だんだん輪郭を成し、姿かたちが見えてくるように思う。如月は女の子だったと、今、文江は確信している。黒いゆたかな髪の、眉の濃い、頬の赤くて丸い、女の子。如月と声をかけると、かならずその子が浮かび上がって文江に笑いかける。

それから一年しても次の子はできなかった。もしや自分が、義母や真一の言いつけを守らず、如月の墓に日参しているからだろうかとときに考えてはおそろしくなるが、しかし文江は墓に参るのをやめられない。昼飯の用意のために畑を離れ、うしろを振り向き振り向きして、逃げるように寺の裏を目指してしまう。

In the mornings, Fumie went out to work in the fields with Shinichi and his mother. Then at midday, on her way home to prepare the meal, she would secretly pay a visit to the grave. The village gravestones were spread here and there around the slope behind the temple. Of course, no stone bore the name Kisaragi, but crouching down, palms together, Fumie called the name out. Kisaragi, Kisaragi, she said softly. Normally, she couldn't think what else to say. Sometimes, though, she would place beside the grave an orange she had picked along the path, sometimes a *renge* flower. And then words would come to her. Eat it, Kisaragi, she might say, or It's pretty, isn't it, Kisaragi? She felt calm when she did this. The child that had not been born seemed gradually to show itself, at first in outline and then in detail, as if emerging from a cloud of smoke. Fumie was now convinced that Kisaragi was a girl — a girl with shiny black hair, dark eyebrows and round red cheeks. 'Kisaragi!' Whenever she called the name, the child would appear, and smile at her.

A year went by, but the next child didn't come. Fumie was sometimes frightened that it might be because she had visited the grave every day, ignoring Shinichi's and his mother's instructions. But she couldn't stop going. When she left the fields to prepare the midday meal, she'd aim straight for the slope behind the temple. As she went, she'd keep looking back over her shoulder, as though she were running away.

さらに季節がひとめぐりするあいだに、村では二人の子が生まれ、ひとりが鬼に食べられた。食べられた子は、真一たちの言うとおり、七人目になる子どもである。

鬼に食べられた子は、生まれなかった子と同様、葬式をしない。その家族は、鬼が戻ってこないよう家じゅうの戸を閉めて、十日間閉じこもらねばならないことを、文江は知ってはいたが実際に見たのははじめてである。二日にいっぺん、交代で村のものが魚や野菜を届ける。当番がまわってきて文江も届け物にいった。雨戸を閉め切った家は不気味に静まり返っていた。風呂敷包みを言われたとおり玄関わきに置き、離れたところからしばらく眺めていたが、扉が開く気配はない。しかしいったん家に戻って、また見にきてみると、家は静まり返ったままだったが風呂敷包みはなくなっていた。鬼が戻ってこないようにしているというよりは、鬼が籠城しているように文江には思えた。

By the time the seasons had come around once more, there were two new babies in the village and one other had been eaten by the demon. The child that was eaten had been the family's seventh, so it was just as Shinichi and his mother had said.

Like those who weren't born, a child who'd been eaten by the demon had no funeral. Its family had to stay inside for ten days, with all their doors and windows shut to keep the demon from coming back. Fumie knew that, but this was the first time she'd seen it happen. Once every two days, one of the villagers would take fish and vegetables to the house. Fumie's turn came to make the delivery. The rain shutters were all closed tight, the house eerily silent. She placed the cloth-wrapped food beside the door as she had been told, and then withdrew. She watched for a while from a distance, but there was no sign of the door being opened. When she returned later the house was as silent as ever, but the bundle was gone. To Fumie it seemed that far from being kept away, the demon was holed up inside.

生まれた二人の子を、文江は見にいった。ひとりは三軒隣の信子が生んだ子で、ひとりは山裾に住む金物屋の夫婦の子である。もしかしてそのどちらかが如月ではないかと文江は思ったのだったが、金物屋の子どもは男の子で、信子の子は女の子だったが、見た瞬間、如月とは違うとわかった。

一度、墓に供え物をしていることがばれて、文江は義母にこっぴどく叱られた。寺に入っていくところを清婆に見られ、清婆が義母にそれを伝えたのだった。果たして義母が墓にいってみると花だの柿だのが供えられている。

「あんなことをしているから次の子がくるにこられないんだ」と言って義母は怒った。「もう二度といくな、このまま子を生めないのだったらこの家から出す」とまで、言った。

やむなく文江は寺には寄らず、その前を通るときだけ、如月、如月、と話しかけた。そう呼びかけると浮かび上がる如月は、今ではふくよかに成長し、もう歩くことができる。

Fumie went to see the two new babies. One had been born to Nobuko, a few houses away, the other to a couple who ran an ironmongery at the foot of the hill. Fumie thought that one of the children might be Kisaragi; but the shopkeepers' child turned out to be a boy, and although Nobuko's was a girl, Fumie knew as soon as she saw it that it wasn't Kisaragi.

Her mother-in-law found out one day that Fumie had been leaving things for the child by the grave. Old Kiyo told her she'd seen Fumie go into the temple. The mother-in-law went to have a look and, sure enough, found flowers, persimmons. She gave Fumie a terrible scolding.

'That's why the next one hasn't come,' she said. 'Don't ever go there again. If you can't have a child, we'll send you away.'

So Fumie couldn't go to the temple any more. But whenever she passed by she would always say: Kisaragi, Kisaragi. And each time she called, Kisaragi would appear. She had grown now. She was plump and could walk.

亡くした子に拘泥していると次の子が生まれないというのはこのあたりの迷信だと文江は信じていたのだが、しかし実際寺の裏に足を運ばなくなって三月目、文江は身ごもった。明くる年の秋に生まれるという。真一も義母も、死んで生まれた子がやっと帰ってきたとよろこんだが、文江にはやっぱり、腹にいる子が如月だとは思えなかった。年が明け春になり、夏が近づき腹の子が動くようになると、ますますそう思った。如月と腹の子は、おなかの蹴り方だってまったく違った。

この子が生まれれば、如月のことは忘れるだろうかと文江は考える。見たかのようにはっきり思い浮かぶ姿は、そのうち淡くなって消えてしまうだろうか。そのほうがいいような気もするし、そうなってはいけないようにも思う。このあいだのことがあるからと、真一も義母も文江を気遣い、文江は毎朝二人とともに田畑にいかなくてもいいようになった。子どもが無事に生まれるまで、家のことをしていろと言われ、日がな一日文江は家にいて、繕いものをしたり、洗濯をしたり、食事の支度をしたりして過ごし、疲れると布団を敷いて眠った。眠ろうと思うといくらでも眠ることができた。

Fumie didn't believe that clinging to a lost child meant you wouldn't have another. She thought that was just a local superstition. Nevertheless, three months after she stopped visiting the graveyard behind the temple, she was with child again. It would be born in the autumn. Shinichi and his mother were delighted, thinking that the child that had been born dead had at last come back. But, of course, Fumie couldn't think the child inside her was Kisaragi. And when summer approached and the baby began to move about, she was more convinced than ever. The two children kicked in completely different ways.

Fumie wondered if when this child was born she would forget about Kisaragi. Would the figure that she pictured so vividly simply fade away? She thought that might be for the best, but at the same time she felt it mustn't happen. Because of last time, Shinichi and his mother let Fumie off going to the fields with them every morning. Just look after the house till the baby's born, they said. Fumie spent all day at home — mending, washing, preparing meals. If she grew tired, she would spread out a futon and sleep. She could sleep on and on.

そうしてあるとき夢に如月があらわれた。

如月は足取りもしっかりし、髪はますます黒く、目には幼児特有の力強さがあった。おかあさん、と如月は文江を呼んだ。如月の声をはじめて聞いた。甘ったるいにおいのするような声だった。おかあさん。如月がもう一度呼ぶので、如月、と文江も呼んだ。如月は笑っている。ふっくらした頬にえくぼがある。

如月、おなかにいるのはおまえではないね。文江は言った。

おなかにいるのはあたしではないよ。如月は答えた。たどたどしいが、思いの外しっかりした口ぶりである。その子は男の子だよ。

そうか。じゃあおまえはどこにいるの。文江は訊いた。

海のそばにいるよ。くけどにいるよ。如月ははきはきと言う。

くけどというのは、真一や義母の言う彼方の世界のようなものだろうかと思いながら、そこにいて、いつかこっちにくることもあるのかい、と文江は重ねて訊いた。

それはあたしにはわからない。やらねばならんことがあるし。まだちいさいのに大人のようなことを言う。

何か訊けば如月がちいさな口で甘いにおいの声で何か言うのがうれしくて、文江は訊きたいことをさがす。目覚める前にもっと会話をしておきたいと、眠りながら思っている。

Kisaragi once appeared in her dreams.

She was walking confidently now. Her hair was blacker than ever and her eyes intense, as young children's are. 'Mam!' she said. It was the first time Fumie had heard her voice, a voice as sweet as honey. 'Mam!' she said again. 'Kisaragi!' said Fumie. Kisaragi was smiling. There were dimples in her chubby cheeks.

It's not you in my tummy, is it, Kisaragi? said Fumie.

It's not me in your tummy, said Kisaragi. She spoke stumblingly, yet with surprising firmness. It's a boy in your tummy.

Oh? And where are you? said Fumie.

Beside the sea, said Kisaragi brightly. In Kukedo.

Fumie thought this Kukedo must be something like the world over there that Shinichi and his mother spoke of.

And will you come here sometimes? she asked.

I can't really say. I've things to do, replied Kisaragi, a little child speaking like an adult.

Fumie was happy that when she asked something Kisaragi would say something in reply, words formed by her little mouth, her sweet voice.

Fumie searched for things to say. I must talk more before I wake up, she thought.

鬼に食われた子はどうなるの。思いついて、訊いてみる。

鬼に食われた子は泣いているよ。なぐさめても、泣きやまないんだ。

あんたは泣いていないの。

あたしだってときどきは泣くけど、でも、泣きやむよ。

食べられたわけじゃないから。

そう。食べられたわけじゃないから。

あんたに会えるかしら。

おかあさんがきてくれるなら、会えるよ。くけどにきてくれるのなら。

目が覚める。暗闇の彼方に天井がゆっくりと浮かび上がる。次第に浮かび上がってくる木目模様を目でなぞりながら、おかあさんとはじめて呼ばれたその陶酔を、文江はしばらく味わう。腹の子が、腹の皮を突っ張るように撫でる。ほかの子が先に自分をおかあさんと呼んだ、そのことに嫉妬しているように思えて文江は笑う。真一の寝息が聞こえる。おかあさん。甘いにおいの広がるような声を、文江は耳の奥にくりかえし響かせる。

What happens to the children who are eaten by the demon? she asked.

They cry. Even if they're comforted, they cry.

Don't you cry?

I cry sometimes. But I stop.

Because you weren't eaten?

Yes. Because I wasn't eaten.

Can we meet?

If you come, we can meet, Mam. If you come to Kukedo.

Fumie awoke. She saw the ceiling gradually emerge from the darkness above her. Her eyes followed the grain of its wood as she savoured the rapture of being called Mam for the first time. The child inside her pushed gently against the flesh of her belly. Fumie smiled to think it might be jealous that another child had called her Mam first. She could hear Shinichi's breathing as he slept. Mam! She let the voice echo and re-echo in her ears, a voice like sweet fragrance spreading through the air.

くけどというのは真一たちが言うような彼方の世界ではなく、鉄道を乗り継いでいった海沿いの町に実際にある場所だと文江に教えてくれたのは、年に数度物売りにくる行商人だった。近く生まれてくる赤ん坊のためのもの、出産に必要なもの、冬支度に必要なものを土間で選別しながら、その遠い町のことを文江は聞く。次第に鼓動が速くなる。生まれなかった、もしくは生まれてもすぐに死んでしまった子らは、そこで石を積み、次に生まれるのをじっと待っていると年老いた行商人は話した。おばあやんはそこにいったことがあるの、と文江が訊くと、あるさ、と答える。あたしがいかないところなんてないもの。西も東も、南も北もいくんだもの。

あたしにもいけるかしら。

いや、その腹じゃあ、無理だろうね。遠いから。手漕ぎの船で海を渡るし。生まれたら、その子をおっかさんに預けていったらいいさ。赤い前掛けとお帽子をあげてきたらいいよ。そこまで言って、行商人はわざとらしく口を閉ざす。ああ、ここいらは、いけないんだったね。そういうことをしたらいけないんだった。あんたの最初の子は、そんな遠いところじゃなくてここにいるんだろ。細く折れた枝のような指で、行商人は文江の腹をつついて笑った。

Kukedo was not the world over there that Shinichi and his mother spoke about. It was an actual place near a town by the sea. You had to change lines, but you could get there on the train. She learnt this from an old pedlar woman who came to the village two or three times a year. Fumie was just inside the house, selecting things for childbirth, for the baby, for winter. The pedlar stood beside her, talking. Fumie's heartbeat quickened as she listened. According to the old woman, Kukedo was a place where children waited — children who hadn't been born, or children who'd died soon after birth. They built piles of pebbles, and waited patiently for another chance to be born. Have you ever been there? asked Fumie. Yes, said the old woman. There's nowhere I don't go — south, north, west, east.

I wonder if I could go.

Not with that belly, you couldn't, said the old woman. It's a long way. And you have to cross the water in a rowing boat. Wait till after you've had the baby, then leave it with your mother-in-law. Take a little red apron and a bonnet as gifts. The woman suddenly stopped. She slowly pursed her lips. Of course, she said, you can't do that 'round here, can you? You can't do that sort of thing. Your first child isn't in a far-off place like that. It's right here. The old woman prodded Fumie's belly with her thin, gnarled fingers and laughed.

いける、と思うと、気もそぞろになる。文江は生まれ育った村と嫁いだこの村しか知らないが、山の向こうに鉄道の駅があり、それがずっと遠くまで連れていってくれることはもちろん知っている。それに乗りさえすれば、如月に会えるのだ。文江は上の空で食事の支度をし、帰ってきた真一と義母と会話し、晩めしをすませ、かわるがわる風呂に入って、眠る。眠る前に、また如月が訪ねてこないだろうかといつも思うが、あれ以来、如月はあらわれない。

そうしてある日、庭に出て洗濯をしていた文江は、頭上に広がる秋の空を見上げ、隅々まで雲がひとつもないと気づく。しゃぼんのついた手を洗い、桶に浸かった汚れものはそのままに、暗い部屋に上がってしまってある紙幣を帯の奥に用心深く入れ、ふらりと家を出る。どこからか雲が出てきたら引き返そう、と言い訳をするように思う。が、幾度見上げても空は一枚の布地のように、動きもしないし変わりもしない。鉄道駅に着くころにはお三時を過ぎていたが、それでもまだ、空は透き通った青一色だった。

Fumie grew restless at the idea that she could go to Kukedo. The only places she knew were the village where she'd been brought up and the village she'd come to as a bride. But beyond the hills was a railway station, and, of course, she knew that the track could take her far away. All she had to do to go and see Kisaragi was climb aboard. Her mind distracted, she prepared the meals, talked with Shinichi and his mother when they came home, had supper, took her turn to have a bath, and went to bed. Before sleeping, Fumie always wondered if Kisaragi would come to visit her. But she hadn't appeared again.

One day, Fumie was out in the garden doing some washing. She looked up at the wide autumn sky and saw not a trace of cloud. She rinsed her soapy hands and, leaving the dirty laundry soaking in a tub, went back into the darkness of her room. She tucked some banknotes carefully under her sash, and slipped away from the house. If a cloud appears from somewhere, I'll go back, she said to herself, as though by way of justification. But however often she looked up, the sky was motionless, unchanging as a stretch of cloth. It was past three o'clock by the time she reached the railway station, but the sky was still a clear and uniform blue.

終点まで乗って、そこから乗り換える。さらにその先で、もう一度乗り換える。そうしたらくけどの最寄り駅に着く。駅からくけどまでは少し歩くと老女は言っていた。乗り換えるときは駅員に訊けばいい。くけどまでの切符を買うに足りるだろうかと、帯に入れた紙幣を頼りなく差し出すが、ちいさなかたい切符とともに思ったより多くが返ってくる。荷物は何ひとつ持たず、文江は列車に乗りこんだ。

ひとつ列車を乗り換えて、窓の外が日暮れ、空が端から藍色に染まりだしたときは、さすがに不安を覚えた。今ごろ真一と義母は帰ってきて、洗濯物が桶に入ったまま、夕飯の支度も何もしておらず、家じゅうさがしてもだれもいないと気づき、心配しているだろう、怒っているだろうと思うと、引き返したほうがいいのではないかと思えてくる。腹の子だって、ひと月待ってくれるかわからない。信子はふた月近く早く生んだと聞いた。明日、生まれようとするかもしれない。次の駅で列車が止まったら下りて、反対の列車に乗ろう、うん、そうしよう。そう思うものの、だんだん窓の外に見たことのないものがあらわれて、文江は夢中でそれらに見入り、下りることも真一のことも腹の子のことも、忘れてしまう。

Stay on till the last stop. Then change trains. At the end of that line, change again. That will take you to the nearest station to Kukedo. From the station you'll have to walk a while. That's what the old woman had said. If you're unclear about which trains to take, ask a station guard. Fumie took a banknote from her sash and timidly held it out at the counter, wondering if it would be enough to get to Kukedo. In return, she received a small, hard ticket and a surprising amount of change. Carrying nothing else, Fumie climbed onto the train.

After she'd changed trains once, daylight faded beyond the window and the indigo of evening started to seep across the sky. She began to feel anxious. Shinichi and his mother would be home by now. They'd find the washing in the tub. They'd see that supper hadn't been prepared. They'd search the house and realise nobody was there. They'd be worried. They'd be angry. Fumie began to think she should turn back. The baby inside might not wait another month. She'd heard that Nobuko's had been almost two months early. It might decide to come out tomorrow. She should get off at the next station and catch a train in the opposite direction. Yes, that's what she'd do. But beyond the window things were appearing that she'd never seen before — more and more things. They fascinated her. She forgot to get off the train, forgot Shinichi, forgot the child in her belly.

まず夜が明るい。橙色の明かりがあちこちで弾け、その下を、ずいぶん多くの人が歩いている。かと思うと、店のずらり並んだ一角を列車は通り過ぎていく。果物が並び本が並び湯気を上げる大釜があり、祭りのように人が歩いている。車窓の光景が明るくなるにつれて、列車はどんどん混みはじめる。窓際の席に座った文江は、文句も言わずぎゅうぎゅうの場所に立つ男女をおそるおそる見上げる。どれほどじろじろ見てもだれも文江に目を向けない。

今まで見てきた、土埃のたつ赤茶けた道や、寺の裏のまばらな墓や、鬼を拒んでかたく戸を閉ざした家が、まったく別世界のもののように感じられる。昔話の光景のように。

空が藍色一色に染まる。いくつか星が瞬いている。あれほどにぎやかだった明かりが、今度は減りはじめ、それとともにぎゅうぎゅうに詰まっていた人も、だんだんといなくなる。窓の外にもう見るものがなくなって、それでも文江は、真一や洗濯物のことを思い出さない。ふいに訪れた眠気にうとうとと目を閉じ、こくりとうなだれてははっと目を開け、切符を強く握りしめる。それを幾度かくりかえす。

The night was so bright. Orange lights flickered and flashed — and all those people walking beneath them! The train passed streets of shops. There were displays of fruits and books, large steaming pots and crowds of people milling around, as though at a festival. The livelier the spectacle outside grew, the quicker the train filled up. Fumie, who was sitting by a window, looked up nervously at the men and women standing nearby, tightly packed and uncomplaining. However hard she stared at them, nobody looked at her.

Everything that she had seen before seemed to belong to a different world — the red dusty road, the scattering of graves behind the temple, the house tight shut to keep the demon away. They were like scenes from an old tale.

The dark indigo had now spread across the entire sky. Stars were shining here and there. The cheerful, bright lights of the town began to fade and the packed crowd on the train gradually melted away. There was nothing now to look at through the window, but still Fumie didn't think of Shinichi or the washing. Suddenly drowsy, she closed her eyes. Her head drooped forward and she awoke with a start, gripping her ticket tightly in her hand. Again and again, she nodded off; again and again, she suddenly awoke.

終点で、また乗り換える。プラットホームに浮かび上がるような時計を見ると、夜更けである。駅員に駅名を告げると、二番線から、もうじき列車が出ると言う。目的地には明日の朝着くという。弁当売りから弁当を二つ買い、文江は二番線に急ぐ。

乗りこんだ列車は、半分ほど座席が埋まっていた。空いている席に文江は座る。

列車が走り出し、文江は弁当を食べた。食べながら車内を見まわすと、女が多い。自分より老いた女、若い女。夫らしき男と座る女もいる。子どもを隣に座らせた女もいる。車内の、ぱちぱちと震える白熱灯の下で、においが漂っているのか、みんなぼんやりとした目を文江の弁当に向けている。

こんな夜遅くに女ばかりが乗っているというのも妙だと文江は考える。あるいは、夜に女が家にいるというのは、自分の生まれ育った村と嫁いだ村だけのことで、町では、こんなふうに女たちは夜な夜な出歩いているものなのかもしれない。見られているだけで弁当が目減りするような気がし、文江は掻きこむようにして弁当を食べ、食べながら、ふと気づく。女たちが見ているのは、自分の弁当ではなく、出っ張った腹であると。文江は目を伏せ、空になった弁当箱を静かに片づける。

At the end of the line, she changed trains once more. A clock loomed over the platform. It was very late. She told a station guard the name of her destination. Platform Two, he said. The train leaves soon. You'll arrive tomorrow morning. Fumie bought two packed meals from a hawker and hurried to Platform Two.

The train was about half full. She found a seat and sat down.

The train pulled out. Fumie began to eat. Looking around, she noticed there were a lot of women on the train. Some were older than her, some younger. Some were with men — their husbands, she supposed. Some were with children. Under the flickering light of white incandescent bulbs, they gazed vacantly towards her food. Perhaps they could smell it.

Fumie thought it odd that so many women should be on a train this late. But perhaps it was just in the villages where she'd lived that women stayed home at night. Perhaps in towns they were out like this the whole time. With all their eyes on her food, Fumie felt that it was shrinking away, so she ate hurriedly, scooping it up into her mouth. But then she suddenly realised. It wasn't her food they were looking at. It was her swollen belly. She dropped her gaze and quietly folded her empty meal box.

大きく点滅したかと思うと、車内の明かりが消えた。真っ暗になり、それから次第に、女の顔の輪郭や窓枠が浮かび上がってくる。目を凝らしてみれば窓の外は星と月でずいぶん明るい。車内は紺色に染まり、その紺にたゆたうように女たちは黙って揺られている。

目を閉じるが、眠たくはならず、しかたなく文江も、見るべきものもないのに目を開けて、暗い車内を見るともなく眺め、列車の揺れに身を任せる。かたたんかたたんと、小刻みに尻が揺れ続けている。はじめてのことに驚いているのか、居心地が悪いのか、腹のなかで赤ん坊がもぞりもぞりと動く。ちいさく幾度もでんぐり返しをしているように。

腹を押さえ、そうして文江は、このなかに入っているのがいのちを持った赤ん坊ではないような気がして、はっとする。ではなんだ、ここに入っているものは。文江は両手を開いて腹をまさぐる。もぞりもぞりしているものは、性別を持ついのちではなく、この先自分が感じるであろうよろこびやかなしみのいっさいであるような気がする。それらが今、ここに詰まって、うごめいているような。

There was a great flash and the lights in the train went out. It was pitch black for a while, but then gradually the outlines of women's faces grew visible, and the shapes of the window frames. Fumie focused her eyes. The world beyond the window was bright under the stars and moon. Inside was now dark blue. The women rocked silently to left and right, swaying in the blue.

Fumie closed her eyes, but sleep didn't come, so although there was nothing to look at, she opened them again. Gazing vaguely into the darkness around her, she abandoned herself to the motion of the train. Her bottom quivered as the carriage rattled along the tracks. Perhaps the unfamiliar vibration surprised the child, or made it uncomfortable. It shifted restlessly inside her, as though it were rolling forwards, around and around.

Fumie pressed her hands against her belly and, as she did so, was astonished to find herself thinking that what lay within was not a living child at all. So what was it? She eased her hands over the surface of her belly, probing gently. This restless, shifting thing inside didn't seem to be a life — a boy or girl; instead, it seemed to be the accumulation of all the happiness and sadness that she would ever know, as though these feelings were all crammed together, seething inside her.

列車が止まり、乗車口が開くが、だれも降りず、だれも乗ってこない。扉が閉まり、また列車は動き出す。星と月に照らされる車内で、女たちは文江と同様にみな眠らない。白目があちこちで鱗のように鈍く光っている。母親に連れられた幼い子どもも、女にもたれかかられた夫らしき男も、しんと黙りこんでいる。かたたん、かたたんと、車輪が枕木を踏む音だけが、響く。文江も目を開いたまま、膨らんだ腹を指を広げた両手で撫でさする。

ほとんどの女が、文江と同じ駅で列車を降り、ようやくこの段になって文江は理解する。そうか、この女たちもみなくけどにいくのか。女たちは改札を出、無言のまま、まばらな列になって黙々と歩く。空は紺よりは薄い青に変わっている。陽が出ていないから、空気が冷たい。指先と鼻先が、もぎれるように痛い。着物の前をかき合わせ、文江は改札をくぐる。
「くけどはこちらでいいんですね」女たちが同じ方向にいくのだからまちがいはないと思いながらも、文江は、すぐ前にいた女に訊いてみた。正しい道を知りたいというよりも、ただ話したかったのかもしれないと、声をかけてから思う。

The train pulled up and the door opened. But nobody got off and nobody got on. The door closed and the train pulled away once more. Inside the train, in the light of the stars and moon, all of the women were awake. Across the aisle, down the carriage, the whites of their eyes gleamed dimly, like fish scales. The little children they'd brought, the men they leant against — all were silent. The only sound was the rattle of the wheels over the sleepers. Fumie's eyes too were open. Fingers spread out, she caressed her swollen belly.

Almost all the women got off the train at the same station as Fumie. It was then that she finally understood. They too were going to Kukedo. Without speaking, the women passed through the ticket gate and walked on, strung out in a silent line. The dark blue of the sky had softened, but the sun was not yet up and the air was cold. Fumie felt its sharp sting in the tips of her fingers and nose. She pulled tight the front of her kimono and went through the ticket gate.

'This is right for Kukedo, isn't it?' Fumie asked the woman in front of her.

Once she'd spoken she wondered if, rather than wanting to know the way, she had just wanted to talk. All the women were going in the same direction, so there wasn't really any doubt about which road to take.

「そうですよ」と彼女は答える。そんなに若くない女である。この人も子をなくしたのだろうかと思うが、そんなことは訊くべきではない。なんとなく並んで歩く格好になる。女は手提げ袋を持っている。膨らんだ袋から風車が飛び出ている。ほかには何が入っているのかと盗み見ると、衣類らしきものと、人形らしきものの髪が見える。

「こちらははじめて？」と、女が訊き、文江は会話ができることに安堵する。

「はい。夢に娘が出てきて、そこにいるって言うもんだから」文江は躊躇なく答えた。

「そういうことも多いようですね」女は小刻みにうなずいている。

「みんなそうじゃないんですか」あなたは、と訊きたいのを、みんな、にして、訊いた。

「私んとこは夢にも出てこないから、どこにいるんだか、さっぱりわかりません。でも、そこにいればすぐにわかると思います。今までいった場所にはいなかった」

'Yes,' said the woman.

She wasn't all that young. Had *she* lost a child too? Fumie wanted to know, but didn't feel she should ask. They ended up walking side by side. The woman was carrying a bulging bag. A toy windmill was sticking out from the top. Fumie peered over to see what else it carried. There seemed to be clothes, and the hair of what must have been a doll.

'Is this your first time here?' asked the woman.

Fumie was relieved to be able to talk and without hesitation said:

'Yes, I dreamt of my daughter and she told me she was here.'

'That seems to happen often,' said the woman, nodding.

'But not with everyone?' Fumie wanted to say 'you', but said 'everyone' instead.

'Mine doesn't come to my dreams, so I don't know where it is at all. But if I'm in the right place, I think I'll know straight away. It hasn't been anywhere I've visited before.'

「じゃあきっと、ここにはいますね」今までいった場所というからには、似たような場所が、ほかにもあるのだろうか。行商の老女はそんなことは言っていなかった。でも、あるのかもしれない。空がさっきよりだいぶ白くなって、はるか先、刀ですっと切れ目を入れたように、橙色になる。切れ目は空を持ち上げるように膨らむ。中心がどんどん丸くなる。空気の冷たさが、ゆっくりと和らいでいく。前を歩く女たちの輪郭が、黄金色に光る。

道の両側に、いくつか店が並びはじめる。数軒がすでに開いている。列がばらけ、幾人かの女たちが店に向かう。もの珍しげに文江は店をのぞく。隣の女が持っているような風車を売る店があり、ちいさな下駄を売る店があり、赤い帽子と前掛けを売る店がある。ああ、供えてはいけないと義母が言っているものだとすぐにわかる。女たちは子どものために買い求めていくのだ。まだ紙幣が残っていることを思い出し、列を離れて店に向かう。なんでもかんでも、ほしくなる。如月はなんでもかんでもよろこぶように思える。先ほどの、痛いような寒さを思い出し、赤い帽子と手袋を買う。買うと、わくわくとうれしくなった。花やみかんを墓に供えるときとは比べものにならないほどのうれしさである。

'Then I'm sure it'll be here,' said Fumie.

Anywhere she'd visited before. Did that mean there were other places like this? The old pedlar woman hadn't said so. But perhaps there were.

The sky was much paler now. An orange line appeared in the distance, as if the sky had been slit with a sword. The slit swelled, as though lifting up the sky above, and at its centre a great circle grew. The chill gradually eased. The women walking ahead were edged in golden light.

There were now shops on either side of the road, some already open. The line grew more ragged as women stopped off to visit them. Fumie peered at the shops with curiosity. One sold toy windmills, like the one her companion had, another, small wooden clogs, another, little red bonnets and aprons. She knew immediately that these were things her mother-in-law would say she mustn't place at the grave. The women were buying them for children. Fumie remembered she still had some money and so she left the line and went to a shop. She wanted every single thing she saw there. Every single thing would delight Kisaragi. Remembering the sharp cold of the morning, she bought a red bonnet and mittens. She was happy and excited when she bought them. She'd been happy when she placed flowers and oranges at the grave, but that happiness didn't compare to this.

列に戻ると、女はとうに先を歩いていた。列の先に目を凝らすと、薄い青が広がっている。海だ、とすぐにわかる。海を渡るのだと、行商の老女はそういえば言っていた。

波打ち際に、いくつもいくつも、お椀のような船が並んでいた。船のわきには必ず男が立っており、女たちは彼らに小銭を渡して次々乗りこんでいく。五、六人ずつ女を乗せると、男はひょいと船に飛び乗り、長細く黒ずんだ艪を操り、丸い船は海面をすべるように進む。

文江も男にお金を渡し、重たい腹を抱えるようにして船に乗りこむ。船底は濡れて、生ぐさい。ともに乗りこんだ女たちは口をきくこともなく、前方を見つめている。船は前後左右に揺れながら、動き出す。風は湿っていて、生ぐさいにおいはどんどん強くなる。はじめて味わう揺れに気分が悪くなり、文江は歯を食いしばって吐き気をこらえる。

十分ほど進んだ先の岩場で、女たちは船を降ろされた。ごつごつと続く岩場の先は洞窟になっている。その暗闇の先にくけどがあるとたしか老女は言っていた。

When she got back to the line the woman she'd spoken to was already far ahead. Beyond the line, she could make out an expanse of pale blue. The sea. She knew straight away. The old pedlar woman had said you had to cross the water.

Along the shore stretched a line of bowl-shaped boats. Beside each one stood a man. Women were giving them coins and climbing on board. Once five or six were in a boat the man jumped in after them and steered it away with his long dark oar. From a distance, the boats seemed to glide across the surface of the water.

Fumie gave a man some money and climbed into his boat, hugging her heavy belly. The floor was wet, and it stank. The other women on board stared straight ahead without speaking. The boat set off, rocking from side to side, back and forth. The wind was humid and the stench grew. Fumie was not used to the motion of the boat, and felt sick. She clenched her teeth to stop herself retching.

After about ten minutes the women disembarked onto some rocks. The rocks were jagged and they stretched towards a cave. Beyond the darkness of the cave was Kukedo. That's what the old woman had told her.

奇妙なことに、洞窟の前に立ってみると、あんなに多くの女たちがお椀の船で先に着いたはずなのに、人の気配がまったくしない。暗いからだろうか、それにしたって……入り口で足を止め、文江は闇に細めた目を凝らすが、いっしょの船だった女たちは、まったく躊躇することなく、次々と洞窟に入っていく。おそるおそる、文江も彼女たちに続いた。

洞窟のなかは、ぬめぬめとあたたかかった。気をつけて歩かないと、濡れた岩場で草履がすべる。でこぼことかたい岩に手を這わせて慎重に足を踏み出す。真っ暗ななかに、剣を突き刺したように細い光が舞い落ちている。そのあたりだけうっすらと明るいが、やはり、先をいった女たちの姿が見えることはない。まるで暗闇に飲みこまれ、咀嚼され尽くしてしまったようだと文江は思うが、それでおそろしくなることはない。もうすぐだ、というような、わくわくした気持ちだけがある。それに呼応するように、子どもの笑い声が聞こえてくる。遠くで鈴を鳴らしているような、澄んだ声だ。子どもの声はどうしてこんなにまっすぐ響くのだろうと、岩の表面を撫でさすって歩を進めながら、文江は思う。奥に進むにつれ、声は近づかないが、重なり合う。ひとりではない、幾人もの子どもたちが笑う声である。それが消えそうになっては重なり、重なってはちいさくなって、ずっと続いている。そのなかに如月の声を聞き

Fumie stood looking in the direction of the cave. It was strange. A lot of women must have arrived already in other boats, but there was no sign of them. The cave was dark, of course, but even so. Fumie paused when she reached the cave mouth, narrowing her eyes to peer inside. But the other women from her boat went straight in with no hesitation at all. Fumie followed them nervously.

The inside of the cave was warm and damp. Unless she trod carefully, her straw sandals would slip on the wet rocks. She ran her hands along the hard, jagged surfaces as she took each cautious step. The deep darkness ahead was pierced by a quivering blade of light. There was a dim patch of visibility where it fell, but no sign of the women ahead. To Fumie, it was as if they'd all been chewed up and swallowed by the darkness. But that didn't frighten her. Fumie was excited. It wouldn't be long now. Just then, as though in answer to that thought, she heard a child's laugh — a clear laugh, like a bell tinkling in the distance. Why do children's voices sound so pure, she wondered, as she fumbled on across the rocks. The voice came no closer as she progressed through the cave, but it seemed to become overlaid by others — not one child now, but several. Their laughter seemed about to fade away, but then the voices surged up again together, then once more grew soft. On and on the voices went, rising up and falling away. Fumie was fretful and impatient, thinking

取ったように思い、文江の気は急く。

次第に、頭上から突き刺さる剣の光が増える。洞窟の奥が透けるように見えてくる。ちいさな入り江があり、入り江の向こうはまた海だ。さっきお椀の船で渡った海は凪いでいたが、こちらは波がある。持ち上がり打ちつけられる波の先端が白く光り、まるで歯のようである。

入り江に出ると、先にいったはずの女たちの姿はどこにもなかった。視線を感じて横を向くと、岩場に沿って無数の子どもがぎゅうぎゅうにかたまって座っていて、文江はちいさく声を上げるが、けれどそれらは子どもではなく、地蔵だった。大きいのもちいさいのも、欠けたのも黒ずんだのもあり、みな、冬場の幼児のように着膨れている。さっき並んで歩いた女が持っていたような風車が、砂浜にも、地蔵のあいだにも、岩場にも刺さっていて、湿った風にいっせいにしゅうしゅうという音をたてまわっている。

she had heard Kisaragi's voice among them.

Little by little, more light from above pierced through the darkness. Fumie could now see across the depths of the cave. She could see out to a narrow, rocky bay and beyond that, the open sea. The water they'd crossed in the round boats had been calm. Here there were waves. The tips of the swelling, crashing water shone white, like teeth.

She went out towards the bay. There was still no sign of the women who should have been ahead of her. She felt eyes watching her, and, turning her head to one side, saw a crowd of children huddled on the rocks. She gasped. But then she realised they weren't children, after all. They were *jizo* statues, stone monk-like figures. There were large ones, small ones; some were damaged or weather-beaten. Each was padded out with clothing, like a child in winter. There were toy windmills too, like the one in the woman's bag. They were wedged in the sand, between the *jizo,* among the rocks. They spun together, whirring in the damp wind.

笑い声はまだ聞こえる。遠くどよめき、波のようにひいては消え、消えたかと思うとまたはじまる。さっき買ったばかりの帽子と手袋を握りしめて、文江は地蔵に近づく。如月はあのなかにいるのだろう。しゃがんで隠れて、笑いを堪えているのだろう。数歩歩いたところで、文江は何かにつまずく。何かが崩れる乾いた音がする。足元を見ると、石がいくつも転がっている。しゃがんだ文江は、すぐ目の前に、石を積み上げたちいさな塔があるのに気づく。ひとつ気づくと、その隣にも、向こうにも、似たような三角錐が数え切れないほど、ある。それが何を意味するのか文江にはわからないが、けれど、今、崩すべきではなかった塔を崩してしまったこと、如月を見つける前に、崩した償いとして倍のふたつ、同じような石の塔を作らなければならないことを、文江はすでに知っている。文江は四つん這いになり、積み上げやすい石を検分しながら塔を作っていく。四つん這いになっても腹がまったく苦しくない。二つの塔を作り上げ、そろそろと立ち上がって、文江は地蔵に近づく。また、別のものを崩してしまう。舌打ちをして、文江はまた四つん這いになる。

There was still the sound of laughter. It surged up like a wave in the distance, then sank away. And just when it seemed entirely gone, it started up once more. Clutching the newly bought bonnet and mittens tight in her hands, Fumie walked towards the *jizo*. Kisaragi is somewhere in there, thought Fumie. She's crouching down, hiding, trying not to laugh. After a few paces, Fumie stumbled. She heard the dry sound of something collapsing. She looked down. Pebbles lay scattered at her feet. She crouched. In front of her was a pile of pebbles, stacked up like a little tower or pagoda. And once she'd noticed one, she saw another right beside it, another over there and there — more than she could count, steep cone-shaped piles. Fumie didn't know what they meant. But she knew already that she had knocked over something she shouldn't, and that before she found Kisaragi she must make amends by building two piles just like it. She went down on her hands and knees, examining which pebbles would be best to use. She started to build a pile. Though she was on all fours, she felt no discomfort with her belly. She completed two piles, slowly stood up and walked on, approaching the *jizo*. Then she knocked over another pile. Clicking her tongue, she sank back down onto her hands and knees.

石を積み上げていく文江の耳のすぐ近くを、澄んだ笑い声が通り抜けていく。顔を上げると、子どもの白い脚が視界の隅をかすめる。如月。如月。おかあさんはきたんだよ。どこにいる。ふざけてないで出ておいで。胸の内でつぶやいて、文江はまた、石を積む。

四つん這いの膝と手のひらが、ほんのりとあたたかくなる。海の水が満ちてきているらしい。ゆるやかな水の流れに、からからと塔が崩れる。ああ、崩れてしまう。文江は片手で体を支え、片手で塔を作り続ける。さっき壊したもの、今崩れたもの。そうしているあいだに、水かさはどんどん増えていく。今や文江の手首も膝も足の甲も、水に浸かっている。それにしてもなんとあたたかくやわらかい水だろうか。そうしたい気持ちに抗えず、文江は体勢を変え尻をついてすわる。うっとりと目を閉じる。笑い声はまだ続いている。耳を澄ますと、それだけでなく、水の満ちる音が聞こえる。しゃらしゃらと、すすり泣く声にも似ている。水泡がはじける音も、石の塔が水にさらわれてゆっくり崩れる音も聞こえる。あたたかくやわらかい水は、文江の腰を包む。あまりの心地よさに文江は立ち上がることを思いつきもしない。目を閉じ、手の触れる石を意味もなく積み上げながら、聞こえる音に耳を澄ます。

As she started to build the next pile of pebbles, a peal of clear laughter rang past her ear. She looked up. A child's white legs flitted across a corner of her vision. Kisaragi! Kisaragi! she said in her breast, putting in place another stone. Mam's here. Where are you? Don't play around. Come out!

Fumie felt a trace of warmth in her palms and knees as she crawled. The tide was coming in. The gentle flow of water eased the pebbles apart. The little tower began to clatter to the ground. Ah! It's collapsing, she thought. Supporting herself with one hand, she carried on building piles of pebbles with the other — the pile she'd knocked over and the pile that had just now collapsed. The water was rising rapidly. Her wrists, her knees, the tops of her feet were submerged. It felt warm and soft. Submitting to impulse, she shifted her position and sat down, her bottom in the water. Blissfully, she closed her eyes. The laughter continued. She listened carefully. She could hear the water rising, like the rustle of weeping. She heard bubbles bursting, piles of pebbles collapsing in the incoming tide. The warm, soft water closed over her hips. She felt so comfortable she did not even think of standing up. Eyes closed, hands pointlessly piling up the pebbles they touched, she listened to the sounds that reached her ears.

閉めきった家は戻ってきた鬼を入れないためじゃないと、唐突に文江は知る。鬼なんかいないのだ、当たり前だ。そんなことだれだって知っている。閉めきった暗い家で、いらない子をひと思いに消しているのだ。どのようにするのか文江は知っていることに気づく。それは自分が消したからか、消されたからか。如月は自分ではないか。私はこれから生まれるのではないか。この腹に、かなしみやよろこびや、ねたみや笑いや、苦しみや許しを詰めこんで、これから生まれていくのではないか。ならばここはどこだろう。文江はなまぬるい水に指を這わせ、ただ触れる石を弄びながら、どのようにしてここまできたかを思い出そうとする。列車に乗った。店の明かりを見た。大勢の男と女を見た。明かりの消えた列車に乗った。尻がずっと揺れていた。女たちが私の食らう弁当を見ていた。いや、見ていたのは腹だ。思い出されるそれらは混じり合い、白熱灯のように点滅する。それほどの遠い道のりを、私は生まれなかった子に会いにきたのだったか、それとも、生まれられずに旅してきたのか。真一と、その母との暮らしが、あの村に嫁ぐまでの記憶が、水に浸かってほろほろと崩れる石みたいに散らばっていく。遠のき、次第に思い出せなくなる。

That house wasn't closed up to keep out the demon. Fumie suddenly knew. There was no demon. Of course there wasn't. Anybody could tell that. Inside that dark, shuttered house they were getting rid of an unwanted child. Fumie realised she knew how to do it. Was this because she'd done it herself, or had it been done to her? Is Kisaragi me? she thought. Is it me that is going to be born? I've packed my belly full of sadness and joy, jealousy and laughter, suffering and forgiveness, and might I now be born? If so, what place is this? Running her fingers through the lukewarm water, playing with the stones, Fumie tried to remember how she got here. She'd taken a train. She'd seen the lights of shops. She'd seen a lot of men and women. She'd taken a train with the lights out. Her bottom was quivering the whole time she was sitting in the carriage. Women were looking at her food. No, it was her belly they were looking at. Fragments of memory jumbled together, flashing like incandescent lights. Had she made that long journey so she could meet a child that hadn't been born? Or had she travelled unable to be born herself? Life with Shinichi and his mother, memories from before she'd come to the village — everything was scattering, like pebbles slowly collapsing in the water. It was all moving farther away, until, gradually, she found she could remember nothing.

文江はおそるおそる目を開ける。乳白色の明かりがあたり一面をのっぺりとさせている。そのなかに大勢の女がうごめいていて、文江は目を見開く。さっき先に船に乗りこんでいった女たちだ。風車を持っていた若くない女もいる。女たちはそれぞれに、赤い前掛けや人形を手に、子の名を呼んでうろうろと歩いている。いくつかの脚が無遠慮に石の塔を崩す。崩したことに気づかずに女たちは歩きまわる。姿は見えないが、子どもの笑い声はずっと続いている。水に反響しながら続くその声は、しかしよく聞いてみれば、すすり泣きのようでもある。自分をさがす母親から、笑いながら逃げているのか、それとも、母と会えず、泣きながらさまよっているのか。膨らんで突き出た腹に両手を這わすが、なかのものはじっと動くことがない。文江は動かない腹を抱え如月と呼んでみる。呼んだのに呼ばれた気がし、文江は思わず応える。おかあさん。おかあさん。風車や玩具や着物を持って歩きまわる母親たちは、けれどその声をかき消すように、子を呼びながら水を弾いて歩き続けている。

Slowly, nervously, Fumie began to open her eyes. She saw a blank of milky light. And in the midst of it, a seething throng of women. She opened her eyes wide. They were the women who'd been in the boats ahead. The woman with the windmill was among them. They wandered about, red aprons and dolls in their hands, calling out children's names. Feet trampled over piles of pebbles, women walking on, unconscious of the damage they had done. Fumie could see no children, but she could still hear their laughter, voices echoing off the water. Or was it the sound of sobbing? Was it children laughing, running from their searching mothers; or were they crying, lost, unable to meet their mothers? Fumie ran her hands over her large, swollen belly. What was inside didn't move at all. She hugged her unmoving belly and called out: Kisaragi! It was she that was calling, but somehow it felt as though she were being called, and so she answered: Mam! Mam! The mothers, with their windmills, toys and clothes, went on walking, splashing through the water, calling out to children, drowning out her voice.

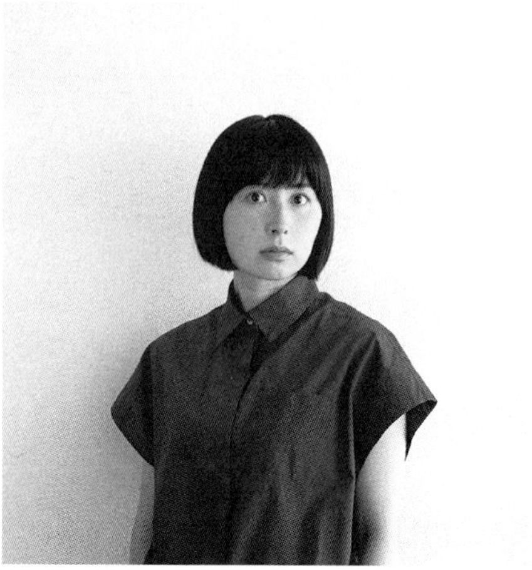

松田青子　Aoko Matsuda

1979年兵庫県生まれ。執筆活動に加え、翻訳家としても活躍。英語で読むことのできる作品としては、初の単著となる『The Girl who is Getting Married（もうすぐ結婚する女）』が2017年に出版されている。「マーガレットは植える」は、2011年の東日本大震災のあと、支援活動の一環として日英両言語で発表された。

Aoko Matsuda was born in Hyogo Prefecture in 1979. Besides writing her own fiction and essays, she is a translator of contemporary English-language literature. The first individual publication of her own work in translation — *The Girl who is Getting Married* — was launched in 2017. 'Planting' was first published in Japanese and English in aid of 2011 tsunami relief.

マーガレットは植える

Planting

松田青子

Aoko Matsuda

マーガレットは植えた。バラの花を植えた。スミレの花を植えた。スズランの花を植えた。シロツメクサの花を植えた。もちろんマーガレットの花も植えた。箱からマーガレットの花が出てきた時、マーガレットは「また会ったわね！」と小さな声でつぶやくと微笑んだ。年月がフェザータッチで描いたなだらかな曲線がマーガレットの目元口元で躍った。マーガレットは植えた。きれいな色の風船を植えた。鼻にこそばゆいようなすっとする香りのリップクリームを植えた。厚みのあるマグカップを植えた。カシミアの靴下を植えた。植えることがマーガレットの仕事だった。だからマーガレットは植えた。派手ではないが、素敵なのを植えた。飽きがこないのを植えた。袖を通したら一日いい気持ちで過ごせそうなのを植えた。やさしい感じの、やわらかい感じの色を植えた。やさしい感じの、やわらかい感じの手触りを植えた。マーガレットは毎日植えた。日々を愛おしむ心を植えた。気に入ったものを長く使う心を植えた。丁寧に扱う心を植えた。マーガレットは急がなかった。マーガレットはゆっくり植えた。ここはゆっくり植えてもいい場所だった。ゆっくり植えてどれだけの時が経っただろう。無造作に毛先がはねているところどころ白いものがまじった薄茶色の髪に、コットン100%のカットソーとズボン、無骨でありながら繊細でもある

Marguerite planted. She planted roses. She planted violets. She planted lilies of the valley. She planted clover flowers. And, of course, she planted marguerites. When she found marguerites in the box, she would smile. 'We meet again!' she would say softly. The gentle curves etched lightly by the years around her mouth and eyes would dance. Marguerite planted. She planted balloons of pretty colours. She planted lip cream, its smell tingling in her nose. She planted thick ceramic mugs. She planted cashmere socks. It was Marguerite's job to plant. And so she planted. She planted lovely things, but nothing grand. She planted things one wouldn't tire of. She planted clothes that would make one feel happy all day. She planted soft, gentle colours. She planted soft, gentle textures. Marguerite planted every day. She planted a heart that knew each day was precious. She planted a heart that kept things it liked and used them time and again. She planted a heart that treated things with care. Marguerite didn't hurry. She planted slowly. It was fine to plant slowly here. How long had she been planting slowly? It was hard to say. Marguerite — her glasses unfashionable but delicate, cardigan and trousers of pure cotton, simple curls at the tips of

フレームの眼鏡をかけたマーガレットとマーガレットの庭を夕暮れの光が淡く包み込んだ。その光景を通りすがりの人が見たら、まるで天国のようだと思ったかもしれない。

マーガレットは疲れた顔でタウンワークをめくっていた。化繊だということを本人も気付いていないまま無頓着に着ている服がちくちくした。ドトールの二階、トイレに一番近い席だった。アイスコーヒーの氷が溶け、グラスがびしょびしょになり、ついでに下に敷かれた紙ナプキンを貫通した水滴でテーブルもびしょびしょになる現象をマーガレットは心底にくんでいたので、いつもは清々しくすぐに飲み干すように心がけていたのだが、毎週月曜日だけはだらしなく水が膨らんでいくのに任せていた。どれだけこんな不毛な日々を過ごしているのだろう。タウンワークの発行日を心待ちに一週間を送る日々だ。毎週月曜日にはファミリーマートでタウンワークをもらい、そのまま通りの向かいにあるドトールでページを開いた。今週こそは自分にぴったりな仕事が見つかるかもしれない。ページを開く前どうしたって一瞬期待してしまう。その希望は薄い冊子を閉じる頃には諦念の混じった絶望に変わる。毎度のことだった。マーガレットはいいかげん気が遠くなりそうだった。求人は毎週ちゃんと更新されていた。新たな求人が生まれて

her white-tinged, light brown hair. Marguerite and her garden, wrapped in the faint light of evening — to a passer-by it would have seemed like heaven.

Marguerite was turning the pages of *Townwork*. She looked tired. Her clothes itched. She didn't care about them; didn't even notice the material was artificial. She was in a Doutor coffee shop, upstairs, in the seat nearest the toilet. Normally she drank her iced coffee quickly. If she waited for the ice to melt, the outside of the glass would become wet with condensation and droplets would seep down through the paper napkin on which it rested and wet the table. She hated that. But on Mondays, she let the water spread messily on the table. Goodness knows how many futile days she had spent like this, week after week, waiting for the next issue of *Townwork*. She picked up a copy at the Family Mart convenience store every Monday, crossed the road to Doutor and started turning the pages. Before looking inside the thin magazine she could never suppress a momentary hope: perhaps this week there would be the perfect job. But by the time she came to close the magazine, this hope had always turned to dejection — dejection mixed with resignation. Every single time. It was too much. Marguerite felt as though she might faint. The jobs were updated every week. There were always new positions advertised. What

いた。不思議なのは歯科医院の助手の募集だった。この世にそんなにたくさんの歯科医院があるのだろうかと訝しく思うほど、毎週湯水のように歯科医院の助手の募集が湧いていた。求人募集を見るのは面白かった。けれど実際問題、マーガレットはどの仕事にもどうしても応募する気になれなかった。「フレンドリーな職場です」と書いてあると駄目だった。フレンドリーな人たちと一緒に働ける気がしなかった。「あなたの夢を応援します」という店長からのエールの横に、頭にバンダナや手ぬぐいを巻き、楽しそうに笑っているバイト仲間たちの写真が添えられていると駄目だった。夢がある人たちと一緒に働ける気がしなかった。客の誕生日が判明した時に、手拍子しながらハッピーバースデーを歌わせられそうな店は駄目だった。作務衣みたいな制服がある店は駄目だった。「頼りになる先輩がしっかりサポート」も駄目だった。今までマーガレットは頼りになる先輩に出会ったことなどなかったからだ。つまりマーガレットは疲れていた。人と関わることに、人と働くことに疲れていた。働くことにはまだ疲れていない気がした。たった一人で誰ともしゃべらなくていい仕事がしたかった。そんな仕事はなかった。けれどマーガレットはある週、ぺらぺらしたページの小さな四角い枠の中にそんな仕事を見つけた。

struck her most were the dental-nurse ads. They gushed out of the pages like water from a spring — it was hard to believe there could be so many dental surgeries in the world. Looking through the ads in *Townwork* was interesting. But the fact was Marguerite never felt like applying for any of the jobs. 'A friendly workplace' — that was no good. She didn't think she could work with friendly people. 'We'll help your dreams come true!' declared a restaurant manager beside a photograph of cheerful young staff, bandanas around their heads. That was no good. She didn't think that she could work with people who had dreams. And she couldn't work in a place where the staff would have to clap and sing if they found out it was a customer's birthday. 'Supportive colleagues' were no good either. Marguerite had never come across a colleague she could rely on. Basically, Marguerite was tired. She was tired of involvement with people, tired of working with people. But she didn't think she was yet tired of work itself. She wanted a job working alone, without having to speak to anyone. There had never been any jobs like that. But one week she found one — on a flimsy page in a small square-framed ad.

最初に箱から出てきたのは真っ白いシャツだった。マーガレットはおそるおそる、でもマニュアル通りにシャツを植えた。シャツをちゃんと植えることができてマーガレットはほっとした。それから箱から出てくるものを一つ一つ丁寧に植えていった。箱は毎日届いた。クロネコで届く日もあれば、佐川で届く日もあった。九時から十八時まで、実働八時間で時給は900円。土日は休みだった。マーガレットは少し時給が安いなと思ったが、すぐに仕方ないと思い直した。何しろ植えるだけの仕事なのだ。それに配達員から箱を受け取るとき以外は、誰とも会わなくていいし話さなくていい。ノルマはなかった。箱の中身をすべて植えきることができなくても、次の日に植えればよかった。だからマーガレットはゆっくり植えた。きれいな音のする陶器の風鈴。色とりどりのマカロン。戦闘美少女のフィギュア。バンドTシャツ。箱からは次々と出てきた。マーガレットは自分の手元にやってきたうつくしいもの、素敵なものを一つ一つ忘れてしまわないようにゆっくり植えた。マーガレットは箱から出てくるものを全部愛おしいと思った。それが何より一番うれしいことだった。

The first thing to come out of the box was a pure white shirt. Marguerite planted the shirt nervously, but in accordance with the manual. She was relieved when she had successfully planted it. And after that she planted, carefully, one by one, each of the other items that came out of the box. A box arrived every day. Some days from Yamato Transport, some days from Sagawa Express. Working time was nine to six — eight hours, allowing for breaks — 900 yen an hour. No work at weekends. At first, she thought the rate of pay was rather low, but she soon decided she couldn't help that. After all, the job was only planting. And she didn't have to meet anyone or speak to anyone apart from the deliverymen who gave her the boxes. There were no performance targets. If she couldn't plant everything from the box one day, she could plant it the next. So Marguerite planted slowly. Lovely tinkling ceramic bells. Macaroons of many colours. Figurines of fighter girls. Band T-shirts. One after another, they came out of the box. And Marguerite planted each one slowly, so that she would not forget any of the wonderful objects that came to her. Marguerite cherished everything that came out of the boxes. That, above all, was what made her happy.

箱から出てきた死んだネズミを見てマーガレットはびっくりした。マーガレットはほとんどつまむようにしながら死んだネズミを植えた。箱からくしゃくしゃになったハンカチが出てきた。マーガレットはくしゃくしゃになったハンカチを植えた。泥水が出てきた。マーガレットは泥水を植えた。休憩時間にマーガレットは近くのスーパーでゴム手袋を買った。ゴム手袋をはめたマーガレットは植えた。ぐっしょりと濡れたぬいぐるみを植えた。しなびた野菜を植えた。羽をもがれた鳥を植えた。赤黒い血が染み付いた絨毯を植えた。マーガレットは箱から出てくるものをまっすぐ見つめることができなかった。何が起こったのかわからなかった。一つの考えが箱から出てくると、それからすぐ後にそれとは正反対の考えが同じ箱から出てきた。一つの思いが出てきた後には、また正反対の思いが出てきた。マーガレットは混乱した。混乱したままマーガレットは植えた。割れたカップを植えた。切り取られた舌を植えた。誰も愛することができない心を植えた。にくしみを植えた。怒りを植えた。埋めたいと思いながら植えた。マーガレットは箱から出てくるものをすべて埋めてしまいたかった。どれだけ芽を伸ばしても地上に到達できないくらい地中深くに埋めてしまいたかった。それができるのはここにいるマーガレットだけなのにマーガレットは

Marguerite was surprised to see the dead rat that came out of the box. She planted the dead rat, holding it away from her, between finger and thumb. A screwed-up handkerchief came out of the box. Marguerite planted the screwed-up handkerchief. Muddy water came out. Marguerite planted the muddy water. She went to a nearby supermarket in her break and bought some rubber gloves. Rubber gloves on, she planted. She planted a soaking wet cuddly toy. She planted shrivelled vegetables. She planted a bird with its wings pulled off. She planted a carpet stained red-black with blood. She could not bear to look directly at what came out of the box. She didn't understand what had happened. As soon as a thought came out of the box, the exact opposite thought would follow. As soon as a feeling came out, the exact opposite feeling would follow. Marguerite was confused. Confused, she planted. She planted a broken cup. She planted a tongue cut out from a mouth. She planted a heart that could love nobody. She planted hatred. She planted anger. She planted, though she wanted to bury. She wanted to bury everything that came out of the box. She wanted to bury it all so deep in the earth that no shoot could ever reach the surface. It was only Marguerite who could bury them. But Marguerite

植えなければならなかった。だからマーガレットは植えた。はやく枯れろと願いながら植えた。枯れろ枯れろ枯れろ。マーガレットは小さな声でつぶやいた。マーガレットの仕事はそういう仕事になってしまった。マーガレットはゆっくり植えることを忘れた。新しい箱が届くと気分が沈んだ。少しでもはやく箱をさばこうとした。でもどれだけ箱をさばいても、以前のようにマーガレットの心が温かくなるような素敵なものは出てこなかった。マーガレットは悲しみを植えた。マーガレットは不安を植えた。マーガレットは後悔を植えた。マーガレットは恐怖を植えた。マーガレットは恐怖を植えた。マーガレットは恐怖を植えた。マーガレットは恐怖を植えた。マーガレットは恐怖を植えた。くる日もくる日もマーガレットは罰ゲームのように恐怖を植えた。今までのように手製の弁当でゆっくり休むこともなく、コンビニのおにぎりを作業の傍らもそもそかじった。マーガレットは深く呼吸することを忘れた。視界が狭くなった。マーガレットは恐怖を取り落とした。あっと思ったマーガレットは我に返った。マーガレットは落とした恐怖を拾うと急いで植えた。気が付くとマーガレットの身体は汗でべたべただった。不快だった。気持ちが悪かった。マーガレットはかつらをとった。こもった熱とともに硬い黒髪が解放された。度数の入っていない眼鏡をとると、顔をこすった。眉墨で書いた皺が斜め

had to plant, and so she planted. She wished what she planted would wither quickly away. 'Wither, wither, wither,' she muttered. That was what her job had become. She didn't plant slowly any more. Her heart sank when each new box arrived. She tried to deal with them as quickly as she could. But however many she dealt with, nothing wonderful now came out — nothing now to warm the heart. Marguerite planted sadness. She planted anxiety. She planted regret. She planted fear. She planted fear. She planted fear. She planted fear. She planted fear. Day after day, she planted fear, as though in a game of forfeit. Instead of relaxing with a home-made lunch, she now ate as she worked, gnawing at a rice ball from a convenience store. Marguerite stopped breathing deeply. Her field of vision narrowed. She took fear from the box and it slipped from her hands. She gasped. As if waking from a trance, she picked up the fear and planted it quickly. She noticed she was sticky with sweat. She was uncomfortable. She felt sick. She took off her wig, releasing trapped heat and with it, stiff black hair. She took off her plain-glass spectacles and rubbed her face. Her wrinkles, drawn in eyebrow pencil, smudged

によれて消えた。何がマーガレットだ。まだ三十年も生きていないくせに、一丁前に疲れたふりの馬鹿な女じゃないか。埋めたいものも植えるしかない女じゃないか。臆病で何もできない女じゃないか。真希子は泣いた。真希子は庭の真ん中に突っ立って泣いた。

(少しだけ昔に森茉莉という作家がいて、彼女は自分のことをマリアと呼んだ。真希子は森茉莉が大好きだった。茉莉さんがマリアなら、自分がマーガレットでもいいじゃないか、誰に迷惑をかけるわけじゃなし。真希子は思った。箱の配達員たちが不可思議な顔と気持ちで真希子のことを見ているのは知っていたが、この職場にいる間、私はマーガレットだ。はじめてシャツを植えたあの日、真希子はそう決めた。)

　真希子は泣きながら庭を見渡した。恐怖が霧のように低く充満した真っ黒な庭は真希子をずぶずぶ呑み込む沼のようだった。ブラックホールのようだった。真希子はどこでもない場所に立っていた。ここはどこだろうと真希子は思った。真希子は気が付いた。最初から選ぶ権利など真希子にはなかったのだ。選べるわけなんてなかったのだ。そりゃそうだ。真希子は小さく笑った。涙はもう出なかった。真希子はかつらをかぶり直した。タオルハンカチで顔をふくと、

diagonally and disappeared. What do you mean 'Marguerite'? A stupid girl, not yet thirty, pretending to be washed out. A girl who can only plant what she wants to bury. A coward, incapable of anything. Makiko cried. Makiko stood crying stupidly in the middle of the garden.

Some time ago there was an author called Mori Mari, who called herself Maria. Makiko loved Mori Mari. She thought that if Mari could call herself Maria, then she, Makiko, could call herself Marguerite. It wouldn't harm anyone, would it? She knew that the men who delivered the boxes looked at her with mystified expressions, mystified feelings, but in this workplace she would be 'Marguerite'. She had decided this on the first day, when she planted the shirt.

Makiko looked around the garden as she cried. Fear hung low in the air, like fog. The pitch-black garden was like a mire, sucking Makiko down. Like a black hole. The place she stood was nowhere. Where is this? she thought. Then she realised — she had never had a choice. There is no way she could have chosen. Of course there wasn't. Makiko smiled faintly. Her tears stopped. She put her wig back on. She wiped her face with a pocket

かばんの中から化粧ポーチを出した。手鏡を見ながら皺を書き直した。眼鏡をかけた。植えてやる。植えてやるとマーガレットは思った。マーガレットは箱に手を差し入れた。恐怖が箱から顔を出した。マーガレットは目をそらさなかった。まっすぐ恐怖を見つめた。そしてゆっくりと恐怖を植えた。きれいに植えた。マーガレットは決めた。私には選ぶ権利がない。でも待つことはできる。ここでこうして植え続けたら、いつかまた素敵なものが、見ているだけで心が温かくなるものたちが、箱から出てくる日が来るかもしれない。ならば私はここで待つ。植えながら待つ。マーガレットは恐怖を植えた。マーガレットは恐怖を植えた。マーガレットは深呼吸した。マーガレットは恐怖を植えた。軽くストレッチして身体をほぐした。水筒に入っているいい香りのハーブティーで一休みした。マーガレットは恐怖を植えた。マーガレットは恐怖を植えた。クロネコの配達員が次の箱を届けに来た。マーガレットは笑顔で箱を受け取った。クロネコの配達員はマーガレットの笑顔をはじめて見たと思った。箱の中身はまだわからない。メンズライクなデザインでちょっとやそっとでは飽きがこない腕時計が終業時間をマーガレットに告げた。マーガレットは明日の箱を明日開けることにした。マーガレットは明日も植える。

towel and took a make-up pouch from her bag. Looking in her hand mirror, she redrew the wrinkles. She put on her glasses. I will plant. I will plant, she thought. She put her hand in the box. Fear appeared. Marguerite did not look away. She fixed her gaze on fear. Then she slowly planted it. She planted it neatly. Marguerite resolved: I do not have the right to choose. But I can wait. If I carry on planting here like this, one day wonderful things may come out of the box again, things it warms the heart just to see. So I will wait here. Keep planting and wait. Marguerite planted fear. She planted fear. She took a deep breath. She planted fear. She stretched a little to relieve the tension in her body. She relaxed for a while with some nice-smelling herb tea from her flask. She planted fear. She planted fear. The man from Yamato Transport brought the next box. Marguerite took it, smiling. The man thought this was the first time he had seen her smile. What was in the box, she did not know. Her watch, a men's style watch that would never go out of fashion, told her that working hours were up. She decided she would open tomorrow's box tomorrow. Marguerite will be planting again tomorrow.

Spot the Difference!

Ten ways in which the translations differ from the original texts

by Angus Turvill (translator)

Translations are at once the same as and different from their original texts. In this commentary, I would like to focus on differences. What kinds of differences are there between these five pieces and their translations, and why do the differences arise?

The layout of the book, with original texts and translations presented side by side, reminds me of spot-the-difference cartoons: two pictures which should be the same, but are different in ten details, say — a crease in a hat, or two birds in the sky instead of three. For this commentary, I won't try to spot every individual difference — there are too many for that — but I will try to identify *ten types of difference* that occur reasonably often.

Some occur where change is inevitable because of grammatical rules, and some where it is made for the sake of readability or clarity. I start with more or less compulsory changes reflecting the grammar of (1) **nouns** and (2) **subjects and objects**. I then discuss (3) **tense** and the (4, 5) **style and representation of speech**. I move on to talk about managing flow through (6) **cutting up and combining sentences**, (7) **switching perspective** and (8) **omissions and additions**. In the final two sections, I talk about handling unfamiliar elements of (9) **culture** and references to (10) **language**.

For each type of difference I give examples showing the Japanese and English versions found in the main text of the book. Where it seems useful I also give an alternative translation, to highlight the issue being discussed. Where such alternative translations are given, the version used in the book is referred to as Translation A and the alternative as Translation B.

When I discuss short expressions in Japanese I give a transliteration, so that all readers can have a phonetic form in mind. I do not do so for longer quotes. Although every example starts with a quotation from the Japanese text, no knowledge of Japanese is required in order to read the commentary overall.

Types of difference

1. Nouns

In certain ways English grammar forces nouns to carry more information than Japanese nouns do. This means that when translating a Japanese noun into English, information may have to be added. This information may include whether an object is singular or plural, general or specific and who owns it.

Singular or plural.

旧式の牛乳瓶、花、茶碗、ミルクポット、食べかけの果物、パンの切れっぱし、首をしめられてぐったりした鳥（'The Otter', p. 30）

A. Translation used in this book: ***old-fashioned milk bottles, flowers, bowls, a milk jug, half-eaten fruit, pieces of bread, a bird with its neck wrung.*** (p. 31)

B. Alternative translation: ***an old-fashioned milk bottle, a flower, a bowl, milk jugs, half-eaten fruit, a piece of bread and some birds with their necks wrung.***

The Japanese here gives a list of items in a picture, but does not specify whether each is singular or plural. Because of grammatical rules, this information has to be added in an English translation. There is no clear basis in the story for a decision, and there is no image available online of a picture as described. The difference between Translations A and B simply relates to whether the nouns are singular or plural, so both seem reasonable versions. In Translation A (the version used in this book), I chose singular or plural for each noun according to how I imagined the picture.

General or specific

> 海のそばの家には、砂がたくさん入ってくる。(**'Summer Blanket', p.74**)
>
> A. **Translation used in this book: *Houses by the sea get full of sand.*** (**p.75**)
>
> B. **Alternative translation: *The house by the sea gets full of sand.***

The word for *house* here in Japanese (家 - *ie*) is not specified as being either general (*houses*) or specific (*the house*). When putting the sentence into English, however, grammatical rules force us to choose one or other interpretation.

Translation A gives the word a general meaning partly because the same Japanese phrase (海のそばの家 - *umi no soba no ie*) is used three paragraphs later with an almost certainly general reference.

However, a purely general interpretation of this first use of the phrase proves awkward in view of what immediately follows. The next clause in the Japanese text (マリウスが砂浜を走りまわってくるせいもある) is about a dog called Marius being partially responsible for the sand problem. It would obviously be unfair on Marius to blame him for the phenomenon of sand in seaside houses in general, so a 'specific' interpretation (*the* house, rather than houses in general) has to be available to the reader. The lack of a systematic grammatical distinction between general and specific in Japanese perhaps means that readers can carry both potential meanings in their minds with no sense of contradiction; but this is impossible in English, where we have to commit fully to one or other interpretation.

To facilitate the combination here of a 'general' reading (sentence 1 in Japanese) with a 'specific' reading (sentence 2 in Japanese), I used a bridging sentence that has no equivalent in the original: *Houses by the sea get full of sand. This is certainly true of mine. Much of it is brought back by Marius...* (p.75)

Possession

指先から煙草が落ちたのは、月曜の夕方だった。('The Otter', p.8) ***The cigarette fell from his fingertips one Monday evening.*** (p.9)

Unlike the translation, the Japanese does not say *his fingertips*. It just says *fingertip(s)* (指先 - *yubisaki*).

In English, however, parts of the body are generally given a possessive determiner (*his, her,* etc.). Adding in a possessive determiner here, in the first sentence of the story, means giving information about both narrative perspective and gender. Because they are not *my* fingers, we know immediately that the narrator and the smoker are not one and the same. Because it is *his* fingers, we learn the smoker's gender. Neither of these pieces of information is clear from the Japanese sentence.

2. Subjects and objects

English finite verbs must have subjects. Objects too must be overtly stated. Japanese verbs, by contrast, can often stand alone. For example in a Japanese equivalent of *I gave it to him,* the elements *I, it* and *him* do not have to appear. A Japanese version might simply be the word for *gave* (あげた – *ageta*). This doesn't mean, of course, that when reading Japanese one is constantly having to guess what's going on. Where such elements are not overtly stated in Japanese, they are normally easily retrievable from the context. But still, they have to be added in translation, and there may sometimes be doubt about what the best choice is. If the subject is first person, it may be unclear whether it should be singular or plural (*I* or *we*). If it seems to be third person, then the translator may have to decide whether it should be *he* or *she*.

Singular or plural

しょっちゅう来るから、('Summer Blanket', p. 88)
'I come here so often, anyway.' (p. 89)

The Japanese verb has no subject here, so to make a grammatical sentence in English a subject must be added. From the context, a choice of either *we* (Omori and Mayuki) or *I* (Omori) would make sense. I chose *I* because the later narrative shows that Omori does sometimes come alone.

Gender

高校のときの先生が、勲章をもらった。同窓会でお祝いを上げることになったので幹事だけでデパートへ下見にゆく ('The Otter', p. 18)
Her old high-school teacher had received an official honour and the alumni were to buy him a congratulatory gift. (p. 19)

From the Japanese text we do not know whether Atsuko's teacher is male or female, but use of third-person pronouns in English means gender has to be assigned. I made the teacher male because this allowed for a less ambiguous sentence — the female determiner *her* relating clearly to Atsuko, and the male pronoun *him,* referring clearly to the teacher.

3. Tense

Although Japanese and English tense inflections are superficially similar, the two languages use their 'tenses' in different ways. Narrative of a single flow of events will often involve a mixture of tenses in Japanese, where English would tend to have tense consistency.

> 私は腕時計を見た。二時半。もうすぐ大森くんが来ることになっている。（'Summer Blanket', p. 78）
>
> A. Translation used in this book: ***I looked at my watch. Two-thirty. Omori would be here soon.*** (p. 79)
>
> B. Alternative translation: ***I looked at my watch. Two-thirty. Omori will be here soon.***

In the Japanese the first sentence is 'past' tense and the second 'non-past' (used for present and future). Translation B keeps the switch of tense, whereas Translation A has both sentences in the past tense.

Mid-narrative shifts from 'past' to 'present' tense in Japanese can signal a change from objective narration to the subjective representation of the real-time experience of a character. Perhaps not retaining this kind of switch entails a loss of that distinction, but for me, such sudden changes of tense in English are distracting and, on the whole, I have gone for tense consistency in these translations.

4. Speech style

Japanese speech tends to give information about speaker gender and status in a way that English speech does not. Certain sentence endings, for example, indicate male speech, and others female speech. Verb forms, meanwhile, can suggest familiarity, superiority, respect or distance. English speech has ways of hinting at such distinctions, but nothing as systematically overt as Japanese does. So certain contrasts and parallels are likely to be lost in translation. Sometimes the loss of contrasts makes it difficult to know who is talking. In such cases it can be helpful to add a speech-reporting clause.

Gender

> 「暑いー。夏みたいだな」
> 「夏よ、もう」（'Summer Blanket', p. 86）
> ***'Whew! It's so hot!' said Omori. 'Like summer!'***
> ***'It*** is ***summer,' I said.*** （p. 87）

In the Japanese, both of these utterances are marked by gender-specific features, male for Omori（だな - *dana*）and female for Michiko（*noun* + よ - *yo*）

In the translation, however, there is no obvious contrast in terms of style of speech. I do not think there is any natural-sounding way of consistently reflecting these distinctions in English.

Respect

> 「御主人ですか？」
> 「先に死んでしまったの。歳が随分離れてたから」（'Summer Blanket', p. 90）
> ***'Is that your husband?'***
> ***'He died. He was much older than me.'*** （p. 91）

The question, from Mayuki to Michiko, uses respect language. Michiko's reply is in a plain style, with no politeness marker. The contrast in speech style reflects the relationship between the older Michiko and the younger Mayuki. Since English does not have systematic distinctions between plain and polite styles of speech, this asymmetry is not maintained in the English translation.

Identifying the speaker

「まぶしいのね」(**'Summer Blanket', p. 100**)

A. **Translation used in this book: *'The sun's so bright, isn't it?' I said.* (p. 101)**

B. **Alternative translation: *'The sun's so bright, isn't it?'***

It is clear from the Japanese sentence ending (のね - *no-ne*) that the speaker is female, and so since Michiko is the only female character present the reader knows that the words must be hers. Because English does not have similar gender marking in speech, a direct translation of the sentence as shown in Translation B would leave the reader unclear about whose words they are. So in the translation used in this book, I decided to add the speech reporting clause, *I said* (Translation A).

5. Speech and narrative

In both English and Japanese, speech can be marked off from narrative (with separate lines and quotation marks), or it can be incorporated into narrative paragraphs. One notable difference, however, is that Japanese does not have a grammatical equivalent of English 'reported speech'. In English reported speech, pronouns and tense are adjusted in the move away from direct speech to fit the narrative perspective — thus ***'I am** going,' he said* (direct speech) becomes *He said* ***he was** going* (reported speech). In Japanese, speech in narrative paragraphs always remains grammatically very similar to direct speech, though politeness features, for example, may be omitted.

Translators from Japanese to English have a choice when handling speech. They can reproduce a direct-style quote, or they can convert it into reported speech. Though direct-style quotes can work well within English paragraphs, sometimes reported speech seems to me to flow more naturally.

> 私を抱いているとき、…いま死ねたらなあ、と言ってくれた。('Summer Blanket', p. 100)
>
> A. Translation used in this book: ***When we made love, he would say he wished he could die just then, as we embraced.*** (p. 101)
>
> B. Alternative translation: ***When we made love, he would say: 'I wish I could die now.'***

Translation B is closer to the direct speech structure found in the Japanese, but in the context of the ongoing paragraph, it seems to me that Translation A reads more smoothly.

6. Cutting up and combining sentences

Cutting up sentences is a major area of change in the translation processes here. Combination of sentences also occurs, though less frequently.

Very often, the objective of dividing sentences is to avoid the unwieldiness that can develop when translating between such structurally different languages. Sometimes the main objective is clarity.

Taking elements out of a long noun phrase to form a separate sentence

This happens frequently. Information that is found as modification of a noun in the original may not fit easily in an equivalent position in the translation. A major factor here is that modification precedes nouns in Japanese, but comes after nouns in English.

> 終りのところがジョーテンカではなくてリョーテンカだと云い張ったサアちゃんと松ちゃんの大喧嘩の時には、タミエさえも意見を求められた。（'Ball', p. 42）
>
> A. Translation used in this book: ***There was once a big argument between Mat-chan and Saa-chan, after Saa-chan claimed the last line was not*** 'jo-tenka' ***at all, but*** 'ryo-tenka'. ***Even Tamie was asked for her opinion.*** (p. 43)
>
> B. Alternative translation: ***At the time of the big argument between Mat-chan and Saa-chan in which Saa-chan claimed that the last line was not*** 'jo-tenka' ***at all but*** 'ryo-tenka', ***even Tamie was asked for her opinion.***

Translation B is consistent with the Japanese in so far as all the information is presented in a single sentence; but to me, the modification of the word *time* feels very heavy in this version. Being presented after the noun, rather than before as in Japanese, it seems to interfere with the sentence's flow of ideas. So in Translation A, the information modifying the noun has been extracted and made into a separate sentence. It seems to me that this division makes the content easier to process for the reader.

Sentence breaks to manipulate order of ideas

Basic differences in structure between Japanese and English mean that a very direct translation often leads to a reversal in the order of ideas. Introducing sentence breaks in translation can be useful in allowing information to be presented in the same order as in the original.

生まれるより先に死んでしまった子に名前などつけてはぜったいにいけない、というのが、その付近での了解ごとだった。('The Child Over There', p. 108)

A. Translation used in this book: ***One must never give a name to a child that dies before it is born. Everyone in the village understood that.*** (p. 109)

B. Alternative translation: ***Everyone in the village understood that one must never give a name to a child that dies before it is born.***

As with the previous example, Translation B maintains the single-sentence structure of the Japanese. However, again, because of differences in grammar between the languages, the information ends up in a different order. In Japanese what comes first is the idea that *one should not give names to such children.* What comes last is the idea that *everyone understood.* In Translation B, the order is reversed, with *everyone understood* coming first and *what* they understood coming after.

To allow the order of ideas in these first lines of the story to be more consistent with the original, Translation A divides the sentence into two.

Breaking long verb sequences

Another situation in which sentence division often seems desirable is when translating a Japanese sentence with a long sequence of verbs. Keeping the same number of verbs in an English sentence can result in a heavy and confusing section of text. I think this is again because of the different structures of the languages. Japanese verbs always come at the end of a clause, so the structure of a sentence tends to be reasonably clear, even if there are a lot of verbs. English clauses, however, can end either with a verb, a noun phrase or an adverbial. This may mean that having too many verbs in an English sentence tends to make the structure awkward to follow.

> 昼飯の用意のために畑を離れ、うしろを振り向き振り向きして、逃げるように寺の裏を目指してしまう。('The Child Over There', p. 112)
>
> A. Translation used in this book: ***When she left the fields to prepare the midday meal, she'd aim straight for the slope behind the temple. As she went, she'd keep looking back over her shoulder, as though she were running away.*** (p. 113)
>
> B. Alternative translation: ***She left the fields to prepare lunch and aimed for the slope behind the temple, looking back over her shoulder, as though she were running away.***

Translation B reflects the single-sentence structure of the original. However, because of the number of verbs, this version feels unwieldy to me. Dividing the text into two sentences, as in Translation A, seems a better option.

Combining consecutive sentences

> 彼らは若くて、きれいなカップルだ。とても仲がいい。('Summer Blanket', p. 90)
>
> A. Translation used in this book: ***They are an attractive young couple, very happy together.*** (p. 91)
>
> B. Alternative translation: ***They are an attractive young couple. They are very happy together.***

Translation B maintains the original's two-sentence structure. Combination of these sentences as in Translation A, however, means repetition of the subject — *they* — can be avoided. In Japanese, there is no problem of repetition as neither sentence has an overt subject.

7. Switching perspective

The same event can be described from different perspectives. For example: *George was bitten by a dog* or *A dog bit George.* I find that flexibility in choice of perspective can be helpful in translating, allowing one to maintain natural expression and to control the flow of ideas. A change of perspective can be achieved through switching grammatical voice (active/passive) or through choice of verb.

Switching grammatical voice

Talking about Michiko's special tea: どうやって作るのかと尋ねられた。('Summer Blanket', p. 86)

A. Translation used in this book: ***Mayuki... asked me how I made it.*** (p. 87)

B. Alternative translation: ***I was asked how I make it.***

Translation B has the verb in the passive voice, in keeping with the Japanese. Translation A, meanwhile, converts the verb to the active voice. To me, using the active voice seems more natural in English here. I feel that keeping the verb in the passive voice would break the flow of the narrative, and give the reader the odd impression that Michiko is reluctant to identify who asked her how she made the tea.

Verb choice

As mentioned in Section 6, very direct translation from Japanese to English will often mean information ends up in a different order to that found in the original text. There, I gave an example of how the original order of ideas can be maintained by dividing sentences. Another way of manipulating the order of ideas is through switching perspective. Here is an example of doing so through verb choice.

海のそばの家には、砂がたくさん入ってくる。('Summer Blanket', p.74)

A. Translation used in this book: ***Houses by the sea get full of sand.*** (p.75)

B. Alternative translation: ***A lot of sand comes into houses by the sea.***

Translation B seems very close to the Japanese in terms of the elements of meaning. The subjects are equivalents (*sand* in English; 砂 (*suna*) in Japanese), as are the verbs (*comes into* in English; 入ってくる (*haitte kuru*) in Japanese). However, the order in which these elements are arranged differs significantly. Having *sand* as the subject in English means that *sand* must come at the start of the sentence. In the Japanese, however, the first element is *house(s)* (家 - *ie*). In order to keep *house(s)* at the start of the sentence in a translation, we have to make it the subject. This is not possible with the verb *come,* but it becomes possible if, as in Translation A, we use the verb *get* instead. Thus, switching perspective, from *sand coming into houses* to *houses getting full of sand,* allows us to reflect more closely the order of ideas in this first line of the story.

8. Omissions and additions

Carrying over equivalents for every lexical element from an original text may make a translation feel cluttered. Sometimes, on the other hand, even a word-for-word translation may feel incomplete. In these situations omissions or additions can be helpful. (Omissions and additions as methods of handling unfamiliar cultural information are discussed in Section 9.)

Elements that are sometimes not directly reproduced in these translations include connectors, adverbs and verb phrases, when specific equivalents would bring limited additional meaning to the translated text.

Omitted connector

そうしてある日、庭に出て洗濯をしていた文江は、('The Child Over There', p. 126) ***One day, Fumie was out in the garden doing some washing.*** (p. 127)

The translation above gives no equivalent of the initial connector 'そうして (*sōshite*)', with the meaning *and then,* or *in this manner.* It seemed to me that such a connector would feel redundant in English. *One day* (equivalent to ある日 - *aru hi*) alone seems to provide a sufficient bridge with the previous paragraph.

Omitted adverb

全体を低い調子で歌っていたって、やっぱり「コー」というところは声を出さない。('Ball', p. 44) ***She wouldn't utter*** ko-, ***even if the song was being sung in a lower pitch than normal.*** (p. 45)

The Japanese includes the adverb やっぱり (*yappari*) with a meaning of *as one might expect* or *in keeping with what has been said already.* I felt that overt expression of this idea was not vital, and in the absence of any succinct and natural-sounding parallel in English, it would be better not to clutter the sentence with a direct translation.

Omitted verb phrase

宅次は縁側に腰かけて庭を眺めながら煙草を喫い、（'The Otter', p. 8）

A. Translation used in this book: ***He was sitting on the veranda, looking at the garden.*** (p. 9)

B. Alternative translation: ***Takuji was sitting on the veranda, looking at the garden, smoking a cigarette...***

It seemed to me that since a cigarette had just fallen from his fingers, it was not vital to include the information that he had been smoking one. So to lighten the load of the sentence I omitted this verb phrase.

Added verb phrase

「凄いじゃないの」

厚子だった。（'The Otter', p. 36）

A. Translation used in this book:

'That's wonderful!' said Atsuko, coming into the kitchen. (p. 37)

B. Alternative translation:

'That's wonderful.'

It was Atsuko.

The Japanese and Translation B are very close semantic equivalents, but, to me, Translation B feels incomplete and confusing in the context. For the reader to get a clear picture in English of what was happening, I felt it was important expressly to add the information that Atsuko came into the kitchen.

9. Culture — adjustments to address knowledge gaps

The authors of the original texts are writing for a readership with whom, having been brought up speaking the same language in the same country, they share a certain bank of knowledge. Readers of the translations will not have all this knowledge. So I think it can be helpful to make adjustments to allow the translations to be understood with ease. Adjustments may include slipping in cultural information or, occasionally avoiding potentially unfamiliar concepts that may distract the reader from the story.

Adding explanation into the text

Adding a few words to the English text can provide translation readers with explanations that readers of the original will not require.

ドトール（'Planting', p. 160） ***a Doutor coffee shop*** (p. 161)

The original text has only the name 'Doutor'. The translation includes the words 'coffee shop', which have no overt equivalent in the Japanese. These are added because whereas Japanese readers will be familiar with the Doutor chain, readers from other countries will probably not be.

お手玉（'Ball', p. 50） ***small, colourful otedama beanbags*** (p. 51)

The original text here has only the word 'otedama'. The translation borrows this word, but also includes a description: 'small colourful ... beanbags'. This allows readers who are unfamiliar with otedama to develop a mental picture.

宅次は起きぬけに朝刊を取りにゆき、('The Otter', p. 12)

A. Translation used in this book: ... ***he got up in the morning and went to fetch the newspaper from the letter box.*** (p. 13)

B. Alternative translation: ... ***he got up in the morning and went to fetch the newspaper.***

The phrase 'from the letterbox' was added in Translation A to prevent readers assuming that Takuji had gone out to a shop to get the newspaper, whereas in the Japanese context home deliveries of newspapers are the norm.

宅次は縁側に腰かけて庭を眺めながら煙草を喫い、妻の厚子は座敷で洗濯物をたたみながら、('The Otter', p. 8)

A. Translation used in this book: ***He was sitting on the veranda, looking at the garden. The sliding screen that separated the house and veranda was open, and Atsuko, his wife, was kneeling in the tatami-matted room inside, folding the washing.*** (p. 9)

B. Alternative translation: ***He was sitting on the veranda, looking at the garden. Atsuko, his wife, was in the tatami-matted room inside, folding the washing.***

Two scene-setting additions are made here in Translation A. First, there is the information about the sliding screen (*The sliding screen that separated the house and veranda was open*). I added this in because a few paragraphs later Atsuko overhears Takuji muttering. It seemed to me that in a Western-style house somebody inside would be very unlikely to catch what somebody was muttering on the veranda outside. I thought that giving the information about the open paper screen would help make the situation sound plausible and allow a more accurate picture of the scene to develop in the reader's mind.

Second, there is the information that Atsuko is kneeling. This is not specified in Japanese. It seemed to me that any Japanese reader would assume from the context that she would be doing so, but that a Western reader might imagine her sitting on a sofa or standing by a table. So, again, I felt that this detail might help build up the picture in the non-Japanese reader's mind.

Avoiding unfamiliar concepts

彼らは二人とも、ブランデーシュガーを知らないと言った。('Summer Blanket', p. 86)

A. Translation used in this book: ***Neither of them had heard of the type of sugar I used.*** (p. 87)

B. Alternative translation: ***Neither of them had heard of brandy sugar.***

'*Brandy sugar* (ブランデーシュガー)' (based on the English words) is an obsolete Japanese product name, which no reader of a translation could be expected to know. It did not seem to me that an explanation of *brandy sugar* would fit well into the text at this point, so I decided that rather than use the product name itself, I would choose a more general expression: *type of sugar.*

細い夏蜜柑の木に、よく生ったものだと思うほど重たそうな夏蜜柑が実っているのがある。結婚した当座の厚子はそんな風だった。('The Otter', p. 20)

At the time of their marriage, Atsuko's figure had been perfect — a slender citrus tree with full, heavy fruit. (p. 21)

The Japanese refers to a particular type of citrus fruit (夏蜜柑 - *natsu mikan*), which might be translated directly as *summer orange*. I thought that few non-Japanese readers would have any clear idea as to what a *summer orange* was like, and that using the less specific term *full, heavy fruit* would communicate a clearer image.

10. Language — when language itself is the focus

Specific words or phrases in the source language are often a point of focus in a text. There may be wordplay, or a comment on use of a particular phrase. This can prove awkward in translation. Semantically equivalent terms in the language of translation may not support similar wordplay. Likewise, a comment on a phrase in one language may not apply to its equivalent in another.

Wordplay

「マーガレットは植える」(**'Planting'** — title).

The Japanese title of 'Planting', 「マーガレットは植える」(*māgaretto wa* (*ha*) *ueru*), literally means *Margaret plants/Margaret will plant,* but it is also a play on the name of the British clothes designer Margaret Howell. As soon as it is translated the wordplay disappears, because clearly *Margaret plants* in English doesn't sound like the name *Margaret Howell.*

Meanwhile, the name of the character has to be the same as that of a flower, since the text specifies that flowers of that name come out of a delivery box (p. 158/9). For this reason, I used the name *Marguerite,* rather than *Margaret,* moving still further away from the wordplay in the original. The overt association with Margaret Howell in the Japanese is thus forfeited in the translation.

文書課長という、出世コースからはずれた椅子も腹が立たなかった。おれの本当の椅子は、この縁側だという気がしていた。('The Otter', p.8)

A. Translation used in this book: ***Nor would he mind his position at work — Administration Manager — a job with no prospects. The only prospect that interested him was the prospect over his garden.*** (p.9)

B. Alternative translation: ***Nor was he irritated by his dead-end seat (isu) at work, Administration Manager. My real seat (isu) is on this veranda, he felt.***

The description in Japanese of the solace Takuji gets from his garden includes use of different meanings of the word 椅子 (*isu*), which can signify both a seat and a position in an organisation. Translation B reflects how the juxtaposition of meanings operates in the Japanese. I did not think that such an attempt to carry over this dual meaning into English would work well, so in Translation A the equivalent of *isu* carries no double meaning. There is, however, an attempt to maintain a similar effect by using dual meanings of the word *prospect*.

Reference to a particular expression

「おだつな」

とたしなめるところだった。

おだつ、というのは、宅次の田舎の仙台あたりで使うことばで、調子づく、といった意味である。

('The Otter', p.24)

'Odatsuna !' he had been about to say. Cut it out ! His family was from northern Japan and it was a dialect expression that hovered on his lips. (p.25)

Takuji is said to have felt uncomfortable at Atsuko's behaviour during his father's funeral. We are told in Japanese that he is about to say おだつな（*odatsuna*）and that this is an expression from Sendai, where his family come from.

Odatsuna means something like *Don't show off,* but if we simply translated it as *Don't show off,* it would be odd then to say that this English phrase was an expression from Sendai. In this case it seemed reasonable to keep the word in Japanese, providing an equivalent English expression by way of explanation later in the same line.

> 「なんじゃ」
> わざと時代劇のことば使いで、ひょいとおどけて振り向いた厚子を見て、宅次は、あ、と声を立てそうになった。（'The Otter', p. 22）
> ***'What is it, my lord?' she said, in the manner of a samurai drama, her face suddenly comical. Takuji almost gasped.*** （p. 23）

In the Japanese here, the narrator comments on Atsuko's way of speaking, saying it resembles that of a character in a historical drama. In the translation, her Japanese utterance なんじゃ（*nanja*）becomes *What is it, my lord?*

Nanja, however, is not something that an inferior would say to a lord — on the contrary, it is something a superior would say to an inferior. But the only way I could think of making her words suggest a Japanese historical drama was to switch her performance to that of inferior, so that she could use the phrase *my lord.* I couldn't think of any English wording that would mean *what?* and at the same time support the image of a feudal superior addressing an inferior.

Reference to language sounds

In the English version of 'Ball' the children play 'their walking version of

Rock-Paper-Scissors' (p.53). In the Japanese the game is referred to as 'Pineapple Chocolate' (パイナツプルチヨコレイト—p.52), after an old confectionery product made by Glico, and is based on the words Pineapple (パイナツプル), Chocolate (チヨコレイト) and Glico (グリコ). If children win, they take as many steps as there are Japanese syllables in whichever of these three words they have chosen. To avoid bogging the story down with an explanation of the Japanese syllable system, I felt it would be better to adapt the game, so that the children use the numbers of letters in the English words *Rock, Paper* and *Scissors.* I considered using the number of English syllables or letters in *Pineapple, Chocolate* and *Glico,* but there seemed too many letters and too few syllables for the game to work well on either basis.

If I was reading this, I would now immediately want to put spot-the-difference to one side and try out the original game of *Pineapple Chocolate.* So for those who are not familiar with the Japanese syllable system, there are (for the purposes of the game) six syllables in *pineapple* (*pa-i-na-tsu-pu-ru*), six in *chocolate* (*chi-yo-ko-re-i-to*) and three in Glico (*gu-ri-ko*). Instead of *paper,* shout *pā* (for *pineapple*), instead of *scissors,* shout *chyoki* (*chocolate*) and instead of *rock* shout *gū* (*Glico*).

❖ ❖ ❖

The above list of ten types of difference is, of course, not comprehensive, but I hope it gives an impression of at least some of the ways in which the Japanese original texts and their translations diverge. As I said at the start, some of the differences are inevitable because of grammar, but most are more a question of what feels right in the context of English. Of course, I want the translations to be faithful to the meaning of the original text, but I also want to be faithful to the target language, and to build a text that flows in a way that appeals to me as a reader, and hopefully, therefore, to others too. In trying to achieve this, I like to feel the freedom to be creative. Exercising creativity is, for me, what makes translation enjoyable, and perhaps it also helps give translations life.

Finally

I would like to thank all of the authors for supporting the idea of this anthology, as well as the Japan Society for making the book possible, especially Heidi Potter, Alejandra Armendariz-Hermandez and Will Upton. I would also like to express my gratitude to Yurika Yoshida, Corinne Quentin and Eiji Shimazaki for their swift and helpful correspondence, Andrew Cavell and Geoffrey Keen for their insightful comments on the English texts, Atsushi Takamura for his endless patience as designer, Anne Newman and Kana Sakurai for their painstaking copy editing and proofreading and Etsuko Okahisa for her indispensable support throughout. I would also like to thank the students on courses I have taught for their insight and enthusiasm, as well as the people of Shizuoka Prefecture and the organisers and judges of the Shizuoka International, John Dryden, Kurodahan and J-Lit translation competitions, which have been a major stimulus to my involvement in Japanese translation.

About the Translator

Angus Turvill is an award-winning translator of Japanese. His work includes *Tales from a Mountain Cave* by leading humourist and anti-militarist Hisashi Inoue, *The Art of Discarding* by decluttering guru Nagisa Tatsumi and *Lion Cross Point,* by 2015 Akutagawa Prize-winner Masatsugu Ono. He lives in Norfolk, UK.

Acknowledgments

'Kawauso' ('The Otter') by Kuniko Mukoda ©Sei Mukoda 1980. First published in *Omoide Toranpu* (Shinchosha Publishing Co., Ltd 1980). Translation by Angus Turvill ©2008/2018. First published in *Comparative Critical Studies* (Edinburgh University Press 2008). English translation rights/Japanese reprint rights arranged with the copyright holder.

'Mari' ('Ball') by Natsuko Kuroda ©1963. First published by Yomiuri Shimbun 1963. Translation by Angus Turvill ©2015/2018. First published in *Comparative Critical Studies* (Edinburgh University Press 2015). English translation rights/Japanese reprint rights arranged with the copyright holder.

'Samā buranketto' ('Summer Blanket') by Kaori Ekuni ©2002. First appeared in *Oyogunoni, Anzen demo Tekisetsu demo Arimasen,* published in 2002 by Home-sha Co., Ltd, Tokyo. Translation by Angus Turvill ©2005/2018. First appeared in *The 5th Shizuoka International Translation Competition Winning Translations,* published by the Executive Committee of the Izu Literature Festival. English translation rights/Japanese reprint rights arranged with Kaori Ekuni through Japan Foreign-Rights Centre.

'Kanata no ko' ('The Child Over There') by Mitsuyo Kakuta ©2011. First published in *Kanata no ko* by Bungeishunju Ltd, 2011. English translation by Angus Turvill ©2018. English translation rights arranged with Mitsuyo Kakuta through le Bureau des Copyrights Français; Tokyo.

'Māgaretto wa ueru' ('Planting') by Aoko Matsuda ©2012. First published in *Shinsai to Fikushon no 'Kyori'* by Waseda Bungaku, 2012. Translation by Angus Turvill ©2012/2018. First published in *Shinsai to Fikushon no 'Kyori'* by Waseda Bungaku, 2012. English translation rights/Japanese reprint rights arranged with the author.

Photography credits: photograph of Kuniko Mukoda ©Jiji Press; photograph of Mitsuyo Kakuta ©Hisaaki Mihara; photograph of Aoko Matsuda ©Taihei Ohara.